The Secret Puppy

and other tales

Other titles in the Pet Rescue Adventures series:

Alone in the Night
Lost in the Storm
Sammy the Shy Kitten
The Secret Kitten
The Missing Kitten
Misty the Abandoned Kitten
The Brave Kitten
Sky the Unwanted Kitten
Lost in the Snow
The Frightened Kitten
Ginger the Stray Kitten
The Kitten Nobody Wanted

A Home for Sandy
Teddy in Trouble
The Rescued Puppy
The Tiniest Puppy
The Scruffy Puppy
Harry the Homeless Puppy
Jessie the Lonely Puppy
Buttons the Runaway Puppy
Max the Missing Puppy

The Secret Puppy
and other tales

by Holly Webb
Illustrated by Sophy Williams

tiger tales

tiger tales

5 River Road, Suite 128, Wilton, CT 06897
Published in the United States 2018

ISBN-13: 978-1-68010-414-1
ISBN-10: 1-68010-414-4
Printed in China
STP/1000/0190/1217

10 9 8 7 6 5 4 3 2

For more insight and activities, visit us at www.tigertalesbooks.com

Contents

The Secret Puppy

Contents

For Zoe

Chapter One
The Camping Trip

Daisy jumped out of the car, looking eagerly around the field. It was the first time she'd been camping, and she was really excited.

"Is this our tent?" she asked her dad, gazing at the big green and red tent they'd parked next to. "It's huge!"

Dad nodded. "The lady on the phone said it can sleep six. So that means you and Oliver can each have a room to sleep in."

"A pod," Oliver corrected him. "They're called pods, Dad."

Daisy rolled her eyes. Just because Oliver had been camping with Cub Scouts, he thought he knew everything. He always thought he was more clever than Daisy, anyway, being a year older than her. Oliver had enjoyed Cub Scout camp so much that he'd begged and begged for them to go camping during the summer. But Daisy didn't mind. Usually they rented a cottage by the seaside, and it was nice to do something different. Riverside Farm had a lot of things to do, and many animals to make friends with. Mom wasn't quite so convinced about tents, though.

She'd finally agreed to camping, but she'd insisted that they went to the kind of campsite where the owners would put up one of their tents for you, if you wanted. Oliver had said that was cheating.

"Pods, sorry, Mr. Camping Expert." Dad lugged one of the big boxes out of the car. They might not have needed to bring their own tent, but there was still a lot of stuff. They'd rented a little gas stove and some cooking equipment from the campsite as well, but they'd had to bring sleeping bags and lawn chairs to sit on. Dad had said he couldn't cope with sitting on the ground for a week. Then there was all the food and clothes. Mom had insisted on bringing raincoats and boots, just in case.

"Can we go and explore?" Daisy asked hopefully. "Look at the river! It runs right by our tent!" She'd known there was a river running through the campsite – the name was a bit of a giveaway – but she hadn't realized they would be camping so close to it. She could imagine curling up to sleep in their tent, hearing the water rushing along. "There's a bridge to get to the rest of the farm. Oh, and look! Ducks! There might even be baby ones. And I have to go and see the horses!"

"I want to go and look at the pool," Oliver put in. "We won't be long, Mom."

Mom shook her head. "Not yet. You can explore soon, I promise. We need to unpack, and then Dad and I will come with you to have a look around. I need to know where you're going to be before I let you take off."

Oliver looked like he was about to argue, but then he sighed and grabbed an armful of sleeping bags out of the car. "Can I have this room?" he asked, unzipping one of the doors off the main living area. The three bedrooms stuck out at the sides and the back of the tent, and there was a sort of open canopy at the front, which they could cook under if it was raining.

"I thought it was called a pod," Daisy said sweetly, dodging the sleeping bag he flung at her. "If you're having that one, can I have this one in the back?"

Dad nodded. "I don't see why not. They're all the same size."

"And that leaves us the furthest away from Oliver and his snoring," Mom pointed out.

Daisy picked up the sleeping bag Oliver had thrown at her (it was hers) and unzipped the door to the back bedroom. It was actually quite big, she realized, feeling surprised. She'd expected the tent to be tiny, but her bedroom even had a back door! She unzipped it and peeked out, smiling to herself as she saw the river running along a few feet behind the tent. She wasn't going to tell Oliver she had her own secret door—he'd want to swap.

Luckily, it didn't take too long to unpack—Daisy didn't have to put her clothes away, since there wasn't anywhere to put them. She spread out her sleeping bag, thinking that she was actually looking forward to going to bed. She'd never slept next to a river before.

"Daisy? Are you ready? Should we go and take a look around?" her mom called. Daisy jumped up, stepped out of the pod, and zipped the door closed behind her.

"Will you be all right, sleeping in there by yourself?" her mom asked a little anxiously, but Daisy beamed at her.

"It's perfect! Why wouldn't I be all right? It's only like having my own room at home, Mom."

Her mom nodded. "I suppose we're very close to you, if you do get nervous."

Daisy giggled. "I could probably reach a hand out of my bedroom door and tickle your feet if I stretched."

"So what should we go and see first?" Dad asked. "There's a little shop that sells ice cream. Should we do that?"

"Ice cream?" Oliver poked his head out of his pod. Daisy nodded eagerly. It was very warm in the tent; an ice cream sounded perfect.

Mom looked at the little map she'd picked up when they'd arrived at the campsite. "Once we've done that, and we've had a quick look around, I don't mind if you two go off on your own, as long as you promise to tell us where you're going and be back when we say."

Daisy smiled. She didn't usually get to go to places on her own, although Oliver sometimes walked to school with his friends now that he was in middle school.

Being at the campsite was like a big adventure.

They walked past lots of other tents on the way to the shop, which was part of the old farm buildings. They'd all been converted now, with a little food shop, and a gift shop, and a craft area that did workshops they could sign up for. Daisy really wanted to try the jewelry one.

There were quite a few other boys around—including a couple about Oliver's age playing football outside a tent close to theirs. But Daisy couldn't see many girls, except for a few little ones. Still, she didn't mind. There was a lot of stuff to do, and she was looking forward to exploring on her own.

"No one brought dogs with them,"

she said to Dad, as they walked along the line of tents. Daisy loved dogs, and she'd thought that there might be a few staying in tents with their owners.

"I don't think dogs are allowed, are they?" Dad said. "I'm sure I read that somewhere on the website. They might frighten the animals, I suppose."

Daisy sighed, and Dad put an arm around her shoulders. "Don't worry, Daisy. There are a lot of other animals here. Don't forget those piglets, and the horses."

Daisy nodded. She *was* excited about the piglets, but a dog to play with would have been even nicer. She'd been trying to persuade her parents that they should get a dog for a while, but it didn't seem to be working. Mom was worried that their yard wasn't big enough, although Daisy was sure that people with much smaller yards than theirs had dogs. Besides, there was a huge park close to their house, so it didn't really matter. But Mom said that wasn't the same.

She'd tried to get Oliver to help her persuade them, but he didn't really care. He already had a pet, a tarantula called Otto that he'd gotten for his ninth birthday. Daisy hated spiders. If Oliver wanted to upset her, he'd open his bedroom door and pretend he was letting Otto out of his tank. It made Daisy scream. That was one of the good things about camping—Otto couldn't come, either. Oliver had left him with his friend Max while they were gone.

Daisy shuddered, just thinking about the enormous spider. How could Mom and Dad let Oliver have such a horrible pet? And Otto was huge. Not that much smaller than a very small dog, really....

"Come on, slowpoke!" Oliver turned to look back at Daisy, as she started to trail behind the rest of the family. "Don't you want ice cream?"

Chapter Two

Meeting the Puppies

"Someone *has* brought a dog; I'm sure I heard it barking as we walked across the yard!" Daisy pulled at her dad's sleeve. "Well, just little dog noises, really —more like whining than barking."

The teenage girl scooping out the ice cream smiled at her. "Those are the puppies you can hear. They're in the stable on the other side of the yard."

"Puppies?" Daisy asked hopefully.

"Uh-huh. German shepherds. My mom breeds them—we've got so much space with all the old farm buildings that the dogs have their own special room. It's the one with the sign over the door that says Riverside German Shepherds."

"Are we allowed to see them?" Daisy said. She loved German shepherds; they were so noble-looking.

"Maybe—you'll have to ask my mom, Julie. You probably met her at the reception desk."

Daisy nodded. The lady who'd given them the map and told them where their tent was—her name was definitely Julie. And she did look a lot like Amy, the girl in the shop, with dark, curly hair. "I'll ask," she told Amy. "Thanks!"

Daisy wasn't usually all that good at asking for things—she was too shy. But for the chance to meet some puppies, she could be brave enough to talk to someone she didn't know.

Once she'd eaten her ice cream, Daisy persuaded Mom to return to the reception area with her, while Dad and Oliver went to look at the climbing wall.

"Hello! Is everything all right? Do you like your tent?" Julie asked them, smiling.

Mom nodded. "It's wonderful. Much bigger than we'd expected." She gave Daisy an encouraging look.

"Would it be okay...," Daisy began. "I mean—please could I see the puppies? Amy said there were puppies."

Julie laughed. "There are. Six of them. They're 10 weeks old now. Do you like dogs?"

"Yes. I'd love to have my own dog. Do you have a lot of them?"

"Usually only Lucy, the puppies' mom, and Sally, her sister. We don't breed very many puppies—just two litters a year. And then we either sell them as pets, or sometimes they go to be working dogs. Many of our puppies are police dogs now."

Daisy nodded. She knew that German shepherds made good police dogs because they could be trained so well. They were used as sniffer dogs, and search and rescue dogs, too.

"Don't they get too big to be pets?" Daisy's mom asked doubtfully.

Julie shook her head, laughing. "No! Well, they are big, I suppose. We have Lucy and Sally in the house with us, when they aren't having puppies and living in the puppy room, and they do take up a lot of the kitchen in their baskets. But to be honest, it all depends on how well-behaved a dog is. If you train a big dog properly, it takes up less room than a small dog!"

It sounded silly, but Daisy knew what Julie meant. Her friend Melissa had a miniature dachshund, who was beautiful but also completely spoiled. Melissa's entire family ran around after her. She definitely took up a *lot* of room....

"I was actually going over to check on the puppies in a minute anyway," Julie said, glancing at her watch. "You can come with me if you'd like."

"Yes, please!" Daisy said eagerly. "Do they need feeding? Puppies need a lot of meals, don't they?"

Julie looked at her in surprise. "I didn't think you had a dog."

Daisy smiled shyly. "Oh, I don't. But I love reading about them. I got a wonderful book all about dogs for Christmas. I've read it four times, and

puppies were all reserved, it was no use.

They'd reached the main yard now, and Julie opened the door to the puppy room. "We converted it especially for the dogs, so that they've got a place to run outside as well. Now that it's so hot, we've been able to leave the door open all the time, so they can get some fresh air. And we take them out into our yard, too."

Just inside the room was a wire pen with a gate in it, and stretched out on a fleece blanket was a beautiful German shepherd. She looked exactly like the photos from Daisy's book, with golden brown legs and ears, and a black face and back. She had huge dark eyes, and she was staring thoughtfully at Daisy. She didn't look fierce—just watchful.

And Daisy could understand why. Tumbling around her were four beautiful puppies, and she was making sure that Daisy and her mom were safe to be around them. The puppies, however, weren't worried at all. They bounced over to the edge of the cage and scratched excitedly at the wire. If they stood on their hind legs, they could almost put their noses over the top. Two more puppies dashed in from the outside area and flung themselves at the wire, too, yapping excitedly.

Daisy's mom laughed. "Oh my goodness. I can see why you have them out here instead of in the house...."

"We do bring them into the house, too, to get them used to being around people and to being careful with the furniture," Julie explained. "But not usually all at once. It's a big old farmhouse, but eight German shepherds are a bit much for any home."

"They're beautiful," Daisy breathed. She'd been expecting the puppies to be cute, and they were, but it still wasn't quite the right word for them. Although they were really soft and fluffy, they didn't have round little puppy faces. They already had long German shepherd muzzles and upstanding ears. They weren't just cute—they were *handsome.*

Then one of the puppies put his head to one side and gazed at Daisy. His ears twitched and wriggled. Daisy laughed and crouched down to get a better look.

"Oh, he's got a floppy ear," she said, wishing she could pet it. The puppy was the darkest of the litter, with pretty brownish-gold fur, and black markings on his face, like a sort of curly T-shape that went over his eyes and down his nose.

Julie crouched down next to her. "Handsome, isn't he? Their ears start to straighten up around now; he's just taking a little longer than the others. Sometimes they're about five months old before their ears stand up correctly."

The puppy seemed to know that they

were talking about him. His brothers and sisters had lost interest in Daisy, and went off to chase each other around the pen and play with the toys that were scattered everywhere. But he stayed by the wire, watching her intently with his dark, intelligent eyes.

"What's his name?" she asked Julie.

"Well, we try not to name them, even though it's difficult sometimes. It's nice if their new owners can choose their own names," Julie explained.

"He looks really clever," Daisy said.

"He *is* sweet," Mom agreed.

Daisy looked up at her eagerly, and Mom shook her head. "Don't get too excited! We couldn't have a big dog like that."

"But—we might be able to get a

dog? Another kind of dog?" Daisy whispered.

"We're thinking about it," her mom admitted. "Dad would really like a dog, and I had a dog when I was your age. She was named Cola. You and Oliver are old enough to be able to take care of a dog now. So maybe we can think about it when we get home...."

"Oh, Mom!" Daisy flung her arms around her mom's neck.

The puppy by the wire looked up at them, wondering what was going on. His floppy ear straightened up for a second, and then flopped over again. The girl looked down at him, and he licked her hand through the wire and made her laugh. He liked her.

Daisy crouched down by the wire again. "I might be able to have a puppy like you," she whispered.

"You can pet him, if you're gentle," Julie told her, and Daisy slowly stretched out her fingers, so as not to scare the puppy, and rubbed his golden fur. She sighed contentedly.

Julie was smiling. “If you want, Daisy, you might be able to help me with socializing the puppies—getting them used to different people before they go to their new homes.”

“Can I, Mom?” Daisy asked hopefully. She had two weeks at Riverside Farm. It was the perfect opportunity to show Mom and Dad what a fantastic dog-owner she would be. She was scratching the puppy behind his velvety ears now, and he was leaning blissfully against the side of the pen.

Mom nodded. “Just don’t get too used to German shepherds, Daisy! I know they’re beautiful, but if we do get a dog, it’ll definitely be something smaller.”

Chapter Three

Baxter's First Walk

The flop-eared puppy galloped across the grass, and skidded to a halt before he landed in the rose bushes—he knew they were prickly. Then he turned around and galloped the whole way back again. All the puppies loved playing out in the yard. Now that they were getting bigger, they spent a lot of time running around. Julie had given them an old football, and his two sisters were fighting over it in the middle of the lawn. He thought about going to join in, but then he spotted a blackbird landing on top of the old brick wall.

The puppy stalked over, his tail wagging from side to side. He hoped that the bird would come down, so he could get a better look. The blackbird stared back, its head to one side, but it showed no sign of coming any closer. The puppy crept toward the bird, and then made a mad little dash up onto the wall, jumping and scratching at the bricks and barking hopefully. The blackbird fluttered its wings in fright, squawked, and flew away.

"I think you have to sneak up on them a little more to catch them,"

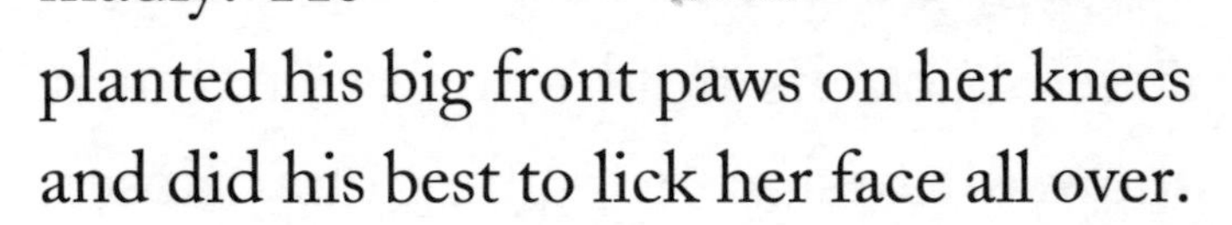

Daisy said behind him. At the sound of her voice, the puppy forgot about the blackbird, and raced over to her, his tail wagging madly. He planted his big front paws on her knees and did his best to lick her face all over.

"Hello there!" Daisy smiled. They were almost a week into their vacation, and she had visited the puppies every day so far. Oliver had been off doing canoeing and raft-building on the river, but although Daisy had gone to a couple of the craft sessions, she by far preferred playing with the puppies.

Daisy's dad had come to find her the day before, and he'd apologized to Julie for Daisy hanging around the puppy pen all the time.

"Not at all—it's great to have someone else to play with the puppies," Julie had explained. "Most of them are going to family homes, so they need to get used to being around children. Daisy's helping me out! And the puppies love her. She's very patient."

Daisy glowed when Julie said that. She really wanted Mom and Dad to think of her as someone who was good with dogs—someone who could be helpful if *they* got a dog. But most of all she was pleased that Julie thought that the puppies liked her. Especially her favorite puppy, the one with the floppy ear. When no one was listening, Daisy had secretly named him Baxter. It seemed to suit him. She did play with the other puppies, too, but Baxter always came over to her and, if she sat down in the pen, he would snuggle up with his nose on her lap. He'd even fallen asleep like that a couple of times.

Lucy, the puppies' mother, wasn't in the pen with them today. She still spent a lot of time with the puppies, but as they were completely weaned from her milk and eating puppy food, she liked a bit of time off now and then. Julie said that all she did when she wasn't with the puppies was rest in her basket, next to her sister, Sally, looking exhausted. Occasionally she'd get up to get a big drink of water. Daisy thought she must be grateful to do this without three or four puppies coming to see what she was doing and then joining in and splashing her.

That morning, Daisy and Oliver had gone for a walk with Dad down to the nearest village, as they both had some vacation money to spend. Oliver had bought a football, and Daisy had spent some of her money on a pack of puppy treats. It was bulging in her shorts pocket now. She'd asked Julie if it was okay to give them to the puppies, and she had said it was fine, as long as it was only a few at a time.

Just then, Julie came up to the door of the pen. "I was thinking, Daisy, if you'd like, you could take one of the puppies out for a little walk around the yard for me," she suggested. "I need them to get used to seeing a lot of people, and walking on a leash, too. They'll all be going to obedience classes as soon as they get to their new homes, and it'll be good if the leash isn't a complete surprise."

Daisy nodded. That would be amazing—like having her very own dog! "Which puppy do you want me to take?" she asked, hoping it would be Baxter.

"You can choose, as long as I know who you've taken—that way I can make sure they all get a turn. Don't take them out of the yard, though, and only walk them for a few minutes. They need to start small and build up."

Daisy glanced at Baxter. She was

sure he would love the yard. He was such a curious little dog. *Maybe people would think he belonged to me*, she thought. He could be her secret puppy, just for a little while.

Julie gave her a collar and a leash to put on Baxter, and showed her how to fasten it so that it would stay on without being too tight.

Baxter wriggled and whined with excitement as Daisy tried to put the collar on him. He wasn't really sure what was happening, but it was definitely new and different. And Daisy was there. He loved it when she came to play with him. She would spend a long time rolling a ball back and forth for him to chase, or stroking his ears.

Eventually Daisy managed to get the leash on him, and she led Baxter out of the pen, and then out the door to the yard, with the puppy waltzing joyfully around her feet. "Careful, Baxter!" Daisy laughed. "You're going to trip me up." She glanced around to check that Julie wasn't listening. She didn't want her to know that she'd named the puppy —he wasn't hers to name, after all.

"We're going on our first walk!"

Baxter stared at the people in the yard, eating ice cream from the shop, visiting the piglets in their stall, or petting the two horses. Children were running around, laughing and shouting. He'd never seen so many people at once. He was used to Julie and the occasional visitor, but that was all. He stopped jumping around and twitched his tail in a nervous sort of wag.

Daisy crouched down next to him. “It’s okay, Baxter. I know it’s a little scary. Let’s just go around the edge of the yard a bit. . . .” She coaxed him along, being careful not to pull on the leash, until they reached a bench. She sat down, snuggling Baxter up against her knees. She wished she could pick him up and have him on her lap, but Julie had told her that the puppies weren’t allowed on the furniture when they went in the farmhouse, because they were going to be just too big when they were older. So she thought it was probably best if he didn’t go on benches, either. But she could still cuddle him. *And* give him a reward, she suddenly remembered!

Daisy pulled the foil pack of treats out of her pocket and tore it open, shaking a few into her hand. "Here, Baxter!" She held them out to him.

Baxter sniffed the delicious treats and glanced around. He'd been staring worriedly at the horse that was leaning its head out of its stall and watching him. It was enormous! But the treats smelled so good that he soon forgot to worry.

He crunched them happily, and Daisy giggled as his soft, whiskery nose nuzzled against her hand, followed by a wet, velvety tongue—Baxter was making sure he hadn't missed any crumbs.

Daisy sat there enjoying the sunshine, and the admiring glances from the people passing by. She knew she should take Baxter back and give one of the other puppies a turn, like Julie had said. But not just yet....

"Daisy!"

Daisy jumped. She hadn't noticed her mom standing beside the bench. She smiled. "Hi, Mom! I didn't see you."

"I was coming to check if you wanted to go to the craft session this afternoon —they're making friendship bracelets. I thought you might like to take some home for Melissa and Eva."

"Okay." Daisy nodded. "That sounds fun. Thanks." She looked sideways at her mom, feeling slightly worried. Why was she frowning like that?

"Daisy, this is the same puppy again, isn't it?" Her mom sat down next to her, and gently rubbed Baxter's floppy ear. He panted happily, enjoying the attention.

"The same as what…?" Daisy said, stalling. She was pretty sure she knew what her mom meant, but she didn't know why it mattered.

"The one with the floppy ear—the one you're always playing with."

"Yes.... But Julie asked me to take him out and show him the yard. It's to get him used to being on a leash."

"And did she say you could give him the treats, too?" Mom asked her.

"Yes! You know I wouldn't feed him anything without asking!" Daisy protested.

"Mmm. But I don't think Julie meant that you should give treats just to this puppy. Have you taken any of the others out like this?"

"No, but...," Daisy trailed off.

"Daisy, if you fall in love with this puppy, what's it going to be like when we go home? We've got less than a week here now, sweetheart. I don't want you to be sad when you have to leave him." Mom sighed. "And actually, it's not very fair to him, either."

Daisy looked up in surprise. "What do you mean? Baxter really likes me! He looks forward to seeing me, I know he does!"

"Exactly. Dogs get very attached to people, Daisy. Next Saturday he'll be waiting for you to come and see him, and you'll be on your way home!"

Daisy's eyes filled with tears. She'd known she was really going to miss Baxter, but she'd been trying not to think about it. He was her vacation dog—her secret, special puppy, just for these few days.

But she hadn't thought about how *he* was going to feel when she was gone.

"You've even named him, haven't you?" her mom said. "You called him

Baxter just now. Julie said she tries not to name the puppies."

"I didn't mean to...," Daisy said quietly.

"I think you need to stop spending so much time with him," her mom told her gently. "He'll be going to his new owners soon. He needs to love them, Daisy. Not you."

Daisy nodded slowly. Mom was right. She'd have to play with all the puppies, not just Baxter, so that he didn't think he was her special one.... Daisy sniffed. She couldn't do it. She knew she couldn't. He *was* special!

She'd just have to stop seeing the puppies altogether.

She stood up, and Baxter followed her, his ears twitching anxiously.

Something was wrong. Daisy's voice had changed, and her eyes looked all shiny. He whimpered, and Daisy patted him, but not the way she usually did. It was almost as though she didn't want to touch him anymore. Baxter laid his ears back and looked up at her worriedly. But Daisy wasn't looking at him.

"I'll take him back," she whispered. "Sorry, Baxter...."

Chapter Four
An Unhappy Pair

Baxter sat by the wire front of the pen, watching the door out to the yard. The top half of the stable door was open, and two of his brothers were dozing in a patch of warm sun, while the others played. But Baxter didn't want to leave his watch to join in. It was hard to tell when someone was going to open the door, because there were footsteps going past all the time, people wandering across the yard to the shop and the craft workshops. But he was listening anyway, waiting for Daisy to come back.

She hadn't been to see him for a long time, and he didn't understand why. Until a couple of days ago, she'd come to the puppy pen every day to cuddle him, or play games with all the puppies. But especially with him. She really loved him; he could tell from the way she looked at him.

It had all changed after they'd gone out for their walk in the yard. He didn't know what had happened, but everything had gone wrong.

Baxter slumped down by the fence, resting his head on his paws and watching the other puppies tumbling around, chasing after a rope toy. Suddenly, his ears twitched. There was a scuffling noise at the door. Was someone coming? Maybe it was Daisy!

The door opened, and Baxter sprang up, jumping at the wire and scratching at it with his paws.

It wasn't Daisy after all—just Julie, with a man and a boy he hadn't seen before. "Oh, that one's excited!" the man said. As soon as he saw them, Baxter dropped down, and stood gazing sadly out through the wire.

"He's a very sweet puppy, very friendly," Julie said, smiling. But as she opened the pen, Baxter slunk away into the corner, leaving his brothers and sisters to get the attention from the visitors.

"I think I saw his picture on the website!" The little boy pointed to Baxter. "He's the one with the floppy ear. Please, can we have him?"

"Is he all right?" the dad asked, as his son crouched down to look at Baxter. "He doesn't look very friendly. Don't get too close, Davey."

Julie was frowning. "He's usually very affectionate," she said.

"Can I pet him?" asked Davey.

Julie smiled. "Of course you can."

But when Davey tried to pet Baxter, the puppy wriggled further into the corner of the pen.

"I don't think he likes me," Davey said sadly. Just then, one of Baxter's sisters rubbed her head against his knees, making him laugh. "But this puppy's nice, Dad!" He sat down on the floor to pay attention to her, and she climbed into his lap, licking his hands excitedly.

His dad laughed. "I think she's chosen you, Davey." He glanced over at Baxter. "I hope the other puppy's okay."

Julie smiled. "I'm sure he's just having an off-day," she said. But she couldn't help feeling surprised. This little one was usually so friendly—maybe he was missing Daisy? Daisy's mom had explained that she thought Daisy was getting too attached to the puppies and it would be better if she didn't spend so much time with them. Julie had agreed—but she hadn't realized that this puppy had already bonded with Daisy, too.

Daisy's mom did all she could to cheer Daisy up, but she wasn't having much success. Everything seemed to remind Daisy of Baxter. She wouldn't go back to see the puppies at all. She said it made her too sad. Her mom almost wished she hadn't said anything, but then the end of the vacation would have been heartbreaking if she'd let Daisy go on falling in love with Baxter.

"I've booked a surprise for you today," Mom told her, as she passed her the box of cornflakes on Wednesday morning. They were just about used to eating in folding camp chairs by now—it was a weird juggling act, trying to pour cereal and milk, and not tip the bowl into your lap. Dad said that if they came camping again, they'd need a folding table, too.

Daisy was pretty sure she *didn't* want to come again. Even to a different campsite. It would remind her too much of Baxter. Still, she was trying not to be upset and ruin the vacation for Mom and Dad and Oliver. "What is it?" she asked, making herself sound interested.

"Horseback riding!" Mom said. "I saw a brochure at the reception area."

"I don't want to go horseback riding, Mom." Oliver looked up from his cereal. "I said I'd go and play soccer with Liam and Tom."

Mom frowned. "Which ones are Liam and Tom?"

"Mo-om!" Oliver sighed. "They're in the red tent at the other end of our row."

"Well, that's good because I didn't book the horseback riding for you anyway." Mom grinned at him. "I didn't think it was your sort of thing. Daisy and I are going together."

Daisy smiled at her. She knew how hard Mom was trying to make her happy. She did love horses, and she'd wanted to try riding for a long time.

"Actually, we should finish up breakfast quickly," Mom said, checking her watch. "We have a reservation for 10."

The stables were about a 10-minute drive from the campsite. Somehow, Daisy felt a little better once they'd driven out of the Riverside gate. She was still really missing Baxter—especially as she kept wondering if he was missing her, too. But she could squash the sadness down inside her, and be just a little bit excited about going to the stables.

The horseback riding was wonderful. Daisy's pony was a gray one named Shadow, who was very well-behaved. He also seemed to know the paths they were taking, so Daisy didn't feel as if she had to worry about where they were going. Mom's chestnut pony, Cracker, was a little more of a handful. She kept trying to stop and eat mouthfuls of grass, which made Mom slide forward. At one point Mom had had to hang on to Cracker's neck to keep herself from falling into a prickly-looking hedge!

Carly, the riding instructor, kept telling Mom to pull Cracker's reins so that she would leave the grass alone. By the time they got back to the stables, Mom told Daisy that she thought she might have pulled her arms out of their sockets!

They helped to rub the ponies down, and they were just saying good-bye when Daisy gasped.

"What's the matter?" Mom asked.

Daisy didn't say anything. She was staring at a beautiful German shepherd, who was standing at the door to one of the stalls. A dark bay horse was leaning out, and it looked as if they were talking to each other.

"That's Frankie," Carly said. "He's our stable dog. Isn't he beautiful? He goes on the rides sometimes, too. He really loves Pepper, the bay horse over there.

If Pepper's out, he follows along." She smiled at Daisy and her mom. "Actually, you're staying at Riverside, aren't you? That's where he came from."

Daisy tried to smile. "Really?" she whispered. Frankie was probably related to Baxter somehow. "Can we go now?" she muttered to Mom.

Mom hugged her. "Of course we can. Oh, Daisy. I'm really sorry...."

All the fun of the horseback riding was swallowed up by how much Daisy was missing Baxter. She was never going to see what he looked like when he was all grown up, like Frankie. She brushed her arm across her eyes to rub away her tears. Why was she being so silly? She'd known all along they'd never be able to take Baxter home. Mom and Dad hadn't even said for sure that they could get a dog, just that they were going to talk about it. And Baxter almost belonged to someone else anyway. But seeing Frankie had made it all seem so much worse.

At least they only had two more days at the campsite. *This was the worst vacation ever*, Daisy thought miserably as she trudged back to the car. And only a couple days ago, she'd thought it couldn't get any better.

Chapter Five

Hiding Baxter

By the next day, Baxter was sick of waiting by the front of the pen. Why had Daisy stopped coming to see him? What if there was something wrong? He prowled around the run all day, sniffing the edges of the pen and trying to find a way out. He needed to go and find Daisy. Hc was surc shc was still somewhere close.

Baxter hardly ate any of the meals that Julie gave him. As usual, she brought the puppies their last meal of the day from the farmhouse at about nine. As she put the bowls down in the pen, Baxter didn't race over like the others. He just went on sniffing carefully at the wire.

Julie shook her head and looked at him worriedly. "I really hope you cheer up a bit before tomorrow," she said, kneeling down next to the puppy to pet him. "Your new owner's coming to see you. She called me today to tell me she's chosen you from those photos I emailed her. She's been waiting for the perfect puppy for a while, she said, and she thinks you're the one. She wants to take you to dog shows."

Baxter nuzzled her hand gently. He might be miserable, but he still liked Julie. He thumped his tail on the scruffy grass of the pen.

"Good boy," Julie said. "Are you missing Daisy? Her mom said she was getting too fond of you, and she was worried it was going to make it hard for her to say good-bye." She sighed. "I probably shouldn't have let her come to see you so much, but she was having such a nice time.... Oh dear, I think that's what it is, isn't it?" She rubbed his ears. "Don't worry. You'll have a wonderful new owner soon."

As she stood up, Baxter sighed and lay down by the wire of the pen, looking out at the yard. Julie frowned. He really *was* missing Daisy. And she was sure Daisy would really be missing him, too.

Julie walked out of the gate, latching it carefully behind her. As she headed back to the farmhouse, she wondered if there was anything she could do to help the puppy.

She didn't notice Baxter's ears twitching curiously. One of them pricked right up, and the other followed suit but then flopped over again the way it always did.

He'd found a hole in the wire fence.

Daisy lay on her tummy at the edge of the river, watching the ducks. Oliver had gone off to play soccer again, and Mom and Dad had gone to wash the dishes after dinner. Daisy thought Mom was probably still feeling sorry for her, after she'd been so upset at the stables. She'd suggested that Daisy read a book in the tent, or find some friends to talk to. But Daisy had spent so much time playing with the puppies that she hadn't really made friends around the campsite like Oliver had.

It was starting to get dark, and the ducks swam slowly away. Dinner had been late—the gas stove had taken a long time to boil the water for the pasta—so it would be time to go to bed soon.

She wriggled up onto her elbows and flicked a little stick into the water, watching it float away downstream. Maybe she could find another stick and race herself.... But then she decided that was just boring. And a bit sad.

I'll go and read in a minute, she thought, dipping her fingers in the water and wishing the ducks would come back.

Baxter scratched at the little dip in the packed earth under the wire fence. The run backed onto the path up to the camping area. If he could just get underneath, he was sure he could find Daisy.

The other puppies were still eating, and his mom was over at the farmhouse, so no one noticed him scraping and digging. Finally, he wriggled underneath the wirc and out onto the path.

He trotted away, sniffing the long grass and wondering which way to go. He could hear people talking—their voices carrying through the quiet evening, as children were called back into the tents, and their parents scttled down to chat for a while before going to bed.

He sniffed again carefully. He couldn't smell Daisy yet, but maybe she would be where he could hear all those voices. He hurried down the path, his tail wagging a little, head down, searching. He could smell the river, although he wasn't sure what it was. It smelled different and exciting, full of the scents of mice and water rats. Then he spotted some ducks, swimming slowly along the far bank, and went faster, eager to get a closer look.

As he was hurrying over the little bridge, he caught Daisy's scent. He stopped dead in his tracks, sniffing the air and looking around hopefully.

She was there! Lying by the water, as though she were waiting for him! He was so desperate to see Daisy that going the entire way to the end of the bridge seemed too slow. With a joyful bark, Baxter jumped through the railings, landing just on the bank, his back paws scratching in the damp mud at the water's edge. Kicking up the mud, he raced along the grassy riverbank and threw himself at Daisy, who stared at him in amazement.

"Baxter! It's you!" Daisy hugged him, laughing. She'd heard the bark, and the loud scuffling and splashing, but she'd never thought it would be Baxter coming to find her. "How did you get here? I wonder if Julie's looking for you—did you sneak out somehow?"

Baxter laid his head on her lap and sighed contentedly. She wasn't angry. Whatever had happened to make her stop coming, she still loved him. He could tell from her voice.

"Oh, Baxter, I've really missed you." Daisy ran her hand gently through the thick fur on his back. "I think you've gotten bigger, and it's only been three days since I last saw you."

Baxter wasn't sure what she was saying, but he liked listening to her.

He wriggled himself closer, so that his paws and shoulders were on her lap, too. He wasn't going to let her disappear again.

Daisy frowned. "I'm not supposed to be around you. Mom says." She swallowed, feeling a lump rising in her throat. "And she's probably right. She thought it was just going to make both of us miserable. I'm going home soon, you see...."

She knew she should take Baxter back to the farmhouse and tell Julie he'd gotten out somehow. But she couldn't. Not just yet. She wanted to cuddle him a little bit longer. Only until Mom and Dad came back from doing the dishes....

But then they might say it was time

for bed, and Dad would take Baxter back instead. Daisy shook her head suddenly. She knew she couldn't let that happen. Mom was right—she was just making it harder for herself, but she didn't care. Being away from Baxter hadn't stopped her from missing him. It didn't look like he'd forgotten about her, either; he'd obviously come to find her. Would another day of being around him really make it any worse for them both?

Daisy gathered Baxter into her arms and stood up. "You're so heavy," she whispered to him lovingly, and Baxter licked her ear. He liked being carried. "Come on. Mom and Dad will be back soon. And Oliver. We're going to have to be a little sneaky."

For just one night she could pretend that Baxter was *her* dog.... Daisy carried him around to the back of their tent, to her own secret door, and put him down beside her while she unzipped it. Then she crawled inside, calling to Baxter to follow her.

He pattered in happily, sniffing around the funny little room, before slumping down on her sleeping bag.

"Good idea," Daisy muttered. "I'll tell Mom and Dad I'm tired. Are you hungry, Baxter?" she whispered, remembering the nearly full pack of dog treats that was still in her pocket.

She hadn't been able to throw it away. "Julie said she usually gives you supper at about nine. Did she leave the gate open afterward?" Daisy frowned. She couldn't imagine Julie doing that. She was so careful. "I know I should take you back, but I can't. Not yet. I'll take you first thing tomorrow."

She fed Baxter a handful of treats, and watched him gulping them down while she put on her pajamas, and slipped into her sleeping bag.

Baxter sniffed thoughtfully around the walls of the tent, and then lay down next to Daisy, staring up at her, his dark eyes glinting in the dim evening light.

Daisy rubbed his head and Baxter wriggled, his ears twitching. Then Daisy heard what he'd heard—voices.

Mom and Dad were on their way back. They mustn't see him!

Quickly, she arranged her fleece blanket half over her sleeping bag and half over Baxter, so he looked like some of her stuff. In this light, when Mom looked in to check on Daisy, she'd never be able to tell there was a dog in there.

"Shhh…," she whispered, feeding him another treat. "You're my secret, okay?"

Baxter scarfed down the treat, and then snuggled closer to her. He didn't mind being quiet, as long as he was with Daisy.

Chapter Six
The Last Night

Daisy woke up early, blinking in the soft sunlight that was coming through the side of the tent. She felt deliciously warm and very happy, but she couldn't quite figure out why.

Then Baxter wriggled and yawned next to her, and she remembered.

"Are you awake, Daisy?" her mom called. "You went to sleep really early last night. Are you feeling okay?"

"I'm fine," Daisy called back, tossing the blanket over Baxter, in case her mom decided to look in and check on her. "Can I go for a walk before breakfast, Mom?"

"I suppose so...." Mom sounded surprised.

"We're going home tomorrow," Daisy added. "I just want to make sure I—um—see everything...."

"You're crazy," Oliver muttered from deep inside his sleeping bag. He hated getting up in the morning.

"I'll be back soon," Daisy promised, flinging on some clothes and unzipping her secret door. Baxter stuck his nose out as soon as she'd opened the zipper enough, sniffing happily at the damp grass.

"Come on," Daisy whispered. "Julie gets up early to feed you. She'll probably have noticed you're missing by now."

She hurried over the bridge, with Baxter pattering after her, his little shiny black claws clicking on the wood.

"Ugh, it's cold." Daisy shivered, wishing she'd looked at the weather before she'd put on her denim shorts. At least she'd brought a hoodie. "I think it might rain," she added sadly. "On our last day." She swallowed. Her last day at Riverside. After tomorrow, she wouldn't be able to see Baxter again.

For a moment, she was tempted to run back to the tent and try to hide him, somehow smuggle him into the car and take him home. But she knew it would never work. It was just a silly daydream.

"Baxter!" she called, hurrying down the path. She wanted to get this over with.

Baxter trotted behind her, his head hanging a little. He could tell where they were going. He didn't want to return to the pen with his brothers and sisters. He'd liked being with Daisy much more.

Daisy had decided she'd better take Baxter to the front door of the farmhouse, as the door in the yard would still be locked. She wasn't quite sure what she was going to say—just that she'd found the puppy. Which was true, even if it wasn't the whole truth. She slowed down as she came up the path, suddenly worrying that Julie might ask her difficult questions.

Baxter hung back at the gate and whined, wishing he were still in the tent. He wanted to snuggle up next to Daisy and have some more of those treats. There was a strong wind blowing, and he didn't like the feel of it whistling around his ears at all.

Daisy came over and picked him up gently. "I know," she muttered in his ear.

"I don't want to leave you, either. But you're not mine, Baxter." She sniffed and knocked on the front door.

It flew open almost at once, and Julie was there with a phone in her hand.

"Oh! He's here. It's all right! Yes, Daisy's got him! I'll call you back in a minute." She ended the call, and hugged Daisy and Baxter. "That was Amy. She'd gone to look along the road for me; we were worried he might have gotten out there. Oh, Daisy, where did you find him?"

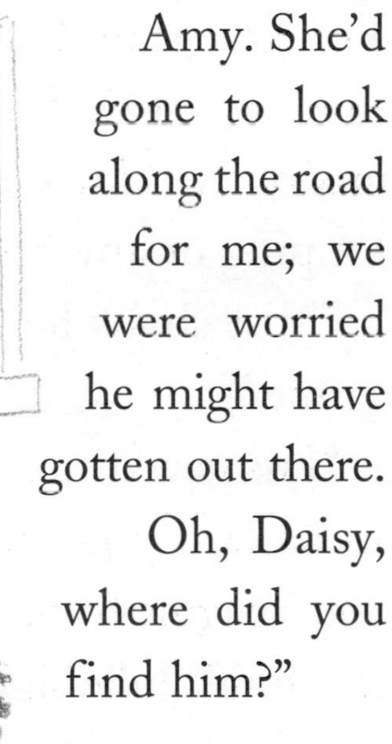

"Um, he found me," Daisy told her. "By the river."

"Thank you so much. I went in to feed the puppies this morning, and realized he was gone. He'd dug a little hole under the wire of the run; I don't know how he squeezed himself out." She patted Baxter gently. "I really thought we might have lost you. I'm going to have to block up that hole, aren't I?" She looked Baxter over anxiously. "He's all right? He wasn't limping or anything, was he?"

Daisy shook her head. "He looks fine to me."

"His new owner is coming to see him today, which just made it all worse—can you imagine having to explain that we'd lost him!" Julie sighed. "At least, I hope she'll be his new owner. I've not actually met her yet, but she sounds very nice."

Daisy nodded, and tried to blink away the tears that had suddenly filled her eyes. "Is she going to take him today?" she managed to ask.

Julie put an arm around her. "No. She just wants to meet him. I'm sure she'll be nice, Daisy. He'll have a wonderful home. And you'll get a dog of your own soon. I told your mom and dad how helpful you were, and how you'd be a terrific dog owner."

"Thanks," Daisy said quietly. But it wasn't the same. She wanted Baxter, and she knew she couldn't have him. Blinking away her tears, she passed the furry bundle to Julie, and Baxter whimpered, wriggling back toward her.

"I'd better go. I just went for a walk before breakfast. Mom doesn't know where I am."

"Come and see us later," Julie suggested. "I want to give you something to say thank you."

Daisy nodded and hurried off up the path.

Baxter stared after her, whining miserably. He'd gone and found Daisy, and she'd been happy to see him. Why was she leaving him again?

"That's really nice of Julie," Mom said, when Daisy explained about going over to the farmhouse later. "You just found Baxter wandering along by the river?"

"Yes." Daisy nodded. She had. She just hadn't been very clear about *when*, that was all. "And so I took him back."

Mom eyed her thoughtfully, and Daisy tried not to turn red as she ate her cereal. She was pretty sure that Mom thought there was more going on than she was telling.

"I'm supposed to be going canoeing on the river this morning," Oliver said dismally, staring out from under the canopy at the dark gray sky. As Daisy walked back from the farmhouse, it had started to rain.

Dad shrugged. "Well, you're going to get wet anyway...."

Oliver made a face. "I know. It just doesn't feel like vacation weather anymore, that's all."

"Maybe it'll blow over," Mom said. But it didn't look like it would.

Daisy walked down to the canoe shed with Oliver and Dad later that morning, while Mom went to the village shops. Daisy was going to go over to the farmhouse once she'd watched Oliver for a little while. It was nice of Julie to want to give her something, but it was making her feel a bit guilty.

It took a while for the canoeing to get started. Oliver had to be given a life jacket and paddle, and told all the safety rules. The instructor kept suggesting that Daisy join in, too. In the end, she told Dad she was going to the farmhouse, just to get away before she was forced into a canoe.

When she went back up to the farmhouse, Julie was already talking to someone—and Daisy gulped, remembering what Julie had said.

It was Baxter's new owner.

Daisy didn't really like the look of her. *That might be because I'm jealous*, Daisy thought, trying to be fair. But it seemed strange that the woman was in a fancy dress, when she was coming to see a litter of muddy-pawed puppies. Her frilly umbrella kept trying to turn inside out, too. Daisy hung around by the gate, trying not to get in the way, but now it seemed as though the woman was leaving.

Julie folded her arms and watched as the woman went down the path. She looked a little annoyed. Daisy wondered whether Julie had discovered that Baxter had stayed in her tent all night. But Julie smiled when she saw her.

"Was that Bax—I mean, the puppy's new owner?" Daisy asked her in a small voice.

Julie shook her head. "No. It should have been. But she's decided she doesn't want him after all."

"Why not?" Daisy stared at her. How could anybody not want him?

"Because of his floppy ear. She's looking for a show dog, you see. It would disqualify him in the show ring."

"But you said he'd grow out of it." Daisy frowned.

"Yes, he probably will. But he's the only one of the litter whose ears haven't straightened up, and she thinks it won't. So—she doesn't want him."

Daisy's eyes widened, as thoughts swirled around her head. "But … does that mean he's still for sale?" she stammered, looking up at Julie in sudden hope.

"Well, yes—there's no one else on the waiting list at the moment, so he is, I suppose. Oh! Daisy, come back, I've got some candy for you!"

But Daisy was gone, racing back along the path to the river, to tell her dad that they had to give Baxter a home.

Chapter Seven

Baxter's Great Escape

"Dad! Dad! You have to come!" Daisy dashed up to where her dad was huddled in his raincoat, watching Oliver, who was out on the river now.

"What's the matter?" Dad looked worried, but Daisy laughed.

"Nothing! Nothing's the matter. It's a good thing! Baxter's new owner doesn't want him. We can buy him!

We could take him home with us tomorrow! You have to come and talk to Julie."

"What? Slow down, Daisy, I don't understand." Dad was frowning, and for the first time since Julie had told her the news, Daisy stopped to think. She'd been so excited that Baxter was for sale again that she hadn't even considered whether her parents would say yes.

"Baxter … the German shepherd puppy—the one I really like. I had to stop seeing him because he was going to belong to someone else, and it wasn't fair to him. But he isn't anyone's now, Dad!"

"What are you two talking about that's so important?"

Daisy jumped. Mom had come up behind her without her even noticing.

"Daisy says that the puppy…," Dad began. He sounded worried.

"It's Baxter, Mom." Daisy's words were tumbling over each other as she tried to explain. "The lady who was supposed to buy him changed her mind. So we can have him—can't we? You said you were seriously thinking about getting a dog. Please, please can it be *this* dog?"

"But Daisy, a great big German shepherd?" Her mom sighed. "I know he's cute and little and fluffy now, but think how big Lucy and Sally are! We couldn't have a dog like that."

"Why not?" Daisy swallowed hard. She couldn't cry now. She needed to persuade them, and they'd never listen if she were crying.

"Well, our yard isn't big enough. The house isn't big enough, either, come to think of it! Imagine a huge dog in our living room, Daisy. He'd take up the entire sofa."

"He wouldn't be allowed on the sofa, Mom. We'd train him properly, like Julie said. So he wouldn't make a mess and stuff. He wouldn't be like Melissa's dog." Daisy dug her nails into the palms of her hands, forcing herself to sound calm and sensible. "There's a dog-training class that meets in the same hall as Brownies. I've seen a poster. And we're so close to the park. I'm almost old enough to take him there on my own."

Her mom shook her head. "I'm not sure about that."

"Well, okay, with Oliver then. And I *will* be old enough soon." She turned to her dad. "You said you wanted to go for walks with a dog, Dad!"

Dad sighed. "I do, Daisy. This is all just a bit sudden. And your mom's right. We never thought of having such a big dog. German shepherds need lots of exercise, and they're bred to be working dogs. I'm not sure they're great pets."

"But you don't know Baxter," Daisy pleaded. "Not like I do. He'd be a wonderful pet." She was losing, she could tell. Mom and Dad didn't understand; they weren't listening. Tears started to stream down her face.

"Don't cry, Daisy." Mom went to put an arm around her, but Daisy pulled away and ran off back to the tent.

How could this be happening?

Baxter could be hers, after all, but she was going to lose him.

Baxter prowled up and down the run, the fur on the back of his neck prickling. He hated being back in his pen, cven though he'd been happy to see the other puppies again. He wanted to be back up at the campsite with Daisy.

Especially now. It was still raining heavily, and the wind was picking up, too. He didn't like the feel of it. It was really howling through the pen, and whistling around the yard, too, rattling all the doors and making the puppies jump and whimper.

He needed to go back to Daisy, and make sure she was all right. But Julie had carefully blocked up the hole under the wire fence, digging a board in so he couldn't get out that way again.

He was stuck.

"You'll just have to share Otto with me instead," Oliver said, grinning. "I'll let you feed him, if you like. Spiders don't need walking all the time."

He was smirking at her over his bowl of soup, and suddenly Daisy couldn't stand it any longer. They'd been stuck in the tent in the pouring rain for a while, and Oliver was driving her crazy. She'd tried being calm and persuasive and sensible, and everyone had treated her like a silly little girl who didn't know what she was talking about.

Okay, fine. So she would be a silly little girl. It didn't matter, anyway. Mom and Dad had refused to listen to any more discussion about Baxter. Mom had said that no meant no, as though Daisy were about three. Mom had even gone to see Julie, and explained that as much as they'd love a dog, they just couldn't have one as big and demanding as a German shepherd.

"I hate you and your dumb spider!" Daisy screamed. She flung herself at Oliver, not even noticing that she'd spilled the tomato soup all down his front. His folding chair tipped over and they both fell to the ground.

"Daisy, stop it!" Mom yelled, and Dad pulled her off Oliver, looking furious.

"Look at you both!" he snapped. "You'd better go to bed, Daisy. And you, too!" he added, as Oliver snickered. "You were teasing her. I'm going to be really glad to get out of this tent and get home tomorrow."

Daisy zipped herself into her pod, changed out of her dirty hoodie and shorts, and crawled into her sleeping bag. She buried her face in the fleece blanket she'd used to cover up Baxter. It still smelled like him. She couldn't stop crying now. She hated it that Oliver and Mom and Dad could hear her. Maybe the drumming of the rain on the tent and the howling of the wind would hide the crying a little.

Baxter was so close. That was the awful thing. Just across the river and down the path. He would be curling up to go to sleep with the other puppies now. She could almost see him….

But they were going home tomorrow, and then she'd never see him again.

Baxter shook his ears worriedly. Julie had closed the door out to the run when she'd come to bring the puppies' dinner because it was raining so hard. But he could still hear it hammering on the roof, and the wind battering around the yard. All the puppies hated the eerie noises.

But he was the only one left awake now. The others had settled into an uneasy sleep, huddled together for comfort. Baxter sat down by the wire fence of the pen and whined miserably. Something was wrong, he was sure of it. All this wind and rain. More than ever, Baxter wanted to be with Daisy. He was scared and she would make him feel better, but that wasn't the real reason he wanted to be with her. He was scared for *her*. The wind had been blowing around the tent even that morning, and he hadn't liked the way it shook. He needed to be there to guard her and keep her safe.

He jumped in fright as a particularly strong gust of wind whistled around the yard and blew the door of the puppy room off its latch. The bottom of the door creaked open, clattering against the wall. It was usually locked at night, but the horrible weather had meant that Julie was racing around, distracted, and she'd forgotten to lock it when she brought the puppies' food from the farmhouse.

The other puppies wriggled and whimpered in their sleep, but none of them woke up. Baxter shivered as the cold wind cut through the room, but then his ears pricked up—or one of them did, anyway.

The door was open now! He could go and find Daisy!

If he could get out of the wire pen....

He scratched at it uselessly, but he only hurt his paws. And it was no good trying to dig under it, as he'd done outside. This was a solid floor. He would have to go over the top of the wire.

Baxter stood on his hind paws, reaching up as far as he could. To his surprise, he was actually as tall as the fence now. His front paws hung over the top, and he could just get his head over it. He kicked and scratched at the floor, trying to push himself up, but he wasn't quite tall enough. Then his claws caught on the bar across the top, and he kicked harder—he was climbing! He scratched again, getting the other back paw up, and heaved himself over the edge of the pen, teetering on the top for a few seconds. Then, almost without realizing how he'd done it, Baxter was on the floor—on the other side of the wire.

He looked nervously at the door. It was still banging back and forth, and it was dark and wet outside. For a moment he wished that he were back inside with his brothers and sisters, where it was warm and safe.

Then he shook himself. He needed to find Daisy. He marched across the floor, and nudged the swinging door hard with his nose.

Out in the yard the rain was

hammering down so hard that he could barely see. Baxter shrank back against the wall, trying to think of how to get to Daisy. When he'd found her before, he'd gone out of the side of the run instead, straight onto the path.

Ears laid back against the driving rain, Baxter set out across the yard to where he thought he remembered the entrance was, his tail tucked between his legs. He'd never seen anything like this before. It had been a hot summer—so hot that all of the ground was dry, and as he reached the path there were huge puddles where the water couldn't soak in fast enough. Baxter hurried around them, shivering as the rain soaked through his thick fur. He was fairly sure he knew where he was going now, but as he came closer to the river his ears laid back even further than before.

It hadn't looked like this yesterday.

The hot weather had left the river low and sluggish, but now the torrential rain had filled it up again, so that it was racing along, sticks and debris jostling around in the dark water. It was starting to overflow its banks, too.

Baxter hesitated at the end of the bridge. Water was lapping around his paws, but he knew that to get to Daisy, he had to go across. The river just seemed so much bigger and scarier now than it had before. It stretched out beyond the bridge on the other side, too, and that was what made Baxter move at last.

On the other side of the bridge was Daisy's tent—and the water had almost reached it.

Chapter Eight
Flood Warning

Baxter raced across the bridge, splashing through the water at the end, which was halfway up his legs. The ground sloped up from the river to the tents, but only a little. The moonlight shone on the dark water that was rising slowly but surely toward Daisy's pod.

He reached the tent and barked as loudly as he could, right outside Daisy's secret door. He hated this water—it was black and scary, and he didn't want it anywhere near Daisy.

Inside the tent, Daisy whimpered and turned over in her sleep as she heard Baxter. The barking just merged into her dreams, making them even more terribly real. Baxter was racing along behind the car as they drove away, barking and barking. He didn't understand why she wasn't taking him with her.

Neither did Daisy.

He was out of sight now. Although Daisy was still staring out of the car window, she couldn't see him at all. So why could she still hear him barking?

Daisy sat up suddenly, clutching her sleeping bag around her. That wasn't part of her dream! That was actually Baxter! He'd come to find her again. Smiling, she unzipped her back door.

"Baxter, shhh! You'll wake up Mom and Dad—oh, wow!" Daisy gasped as she saw the floodwater rising up toward the tent.

Baxter whined impatiently. Why was she still sitting there? She needed to get out, and the others, too! He darted into her tent pod and grabbed her sleeve in his teeth, pulling her.

"Baxter, you came to rescue us!" Daisy whispered, staring at him in amazement. "How did you know? Okay, okay." She reached out to unzip her front door, the one that led into the living area. "Mom! Dad! Oliver! The river's flooding! We have to get out of the tent!"

"What?" There was a scuffling noise, then the zipper opened and Dad's head appeared around the door.

"It really is! Baxter came to tell us, Dad. He's outside. He barked to wake me up!"

Dad dashed across the living area into Daisy's pod, and stared out silently for a moment. Then he turned around and dashed back, grabbing his boots. "I don't how that dog knew, or how he got here, but it's lucky he did. Your mom's just getting dressed. The water will be in the tent any minute. Oliver, up, now! We need to get out of the tent!"

"Where are we going?" Daisy asked, padding across the living area to grab her boots and raincoat.

Dad frowned. "The farmhouse. We need to let them know the river's flooding. I'm sure they'll find somewhere for us to sleep. And help us get our stuff out, too. But I'm going to go and tell the people in the tents closest first." He hurried out, pulling on his raincoat over his pajamas as he unzipped the front of the tent.

Baxter was standing in the doorway of Daisy's pod, watching anxiously. He wanted her out of there now, before that black water came any closer.

"He really came to tell you what was happening?" Oliver said as he struggled out of his pod, still sounding sleepy.

Daisy nodded proudly. "He must have gotten out of the puppy room again."

"That's amazing." Oliver patted Baxter, but he hardly noticed. The water was getting closer and closer. He barked warningly at Daisy, and pulled at the leg of her pajamas with his teeth.

"He wants you to get out of here," Mom said, appearing from her pod. "Get your boots on, Oliver. We'd better go."

Daisy patted her leg and stepped outside. "Come on, Baxter."

It was eerie watching the water creeping up the grass toward the tents. Dad had woken up the families in all the tents closest to the water, and they were starting to come out, dressed in boots and raincoats.

Baxter stood in front of Daisy's tent, looking nervously at the water. They needed to get back across the bridge, but he hated the thought of going across the flooded bank. It would be high up his legs by now. He glanced up at Daisy, her face white in the darkness. She looked scared, too. He whined and took a couple of steps toward the bridge. He had to get her to the farmhouse, where she'd be safe.

Dad came hurrying back with his flashlight. “Good dog. We’re coming now.”

Daisy could hear the other families coming along behind him, the children pointing Baxter out as the dog who’d woken everyone up to rescue them.

“Is he your dog?” one of the boys Oliver played soccer with asked her admiringly.

Daisy caught her breath, staring hopefully up at her dad. He nodded. “After this, I think he is,” he muttered. “I don’t care how big he’s going to get. He’s a hero.”

“They’re trained to be rescue dogs, aren’t they?” Mom said. “I can see why. Come on. We’ll figure out how we’re going to manage when we’re back on dry land.”

Daisy put her hand on Baxter's back. *Her* puppy's back. Dad was holding her other hand tightly, as though he didn't want to let her go.

Baxter looked up at Daisy, and splashed forward into the water, head down, determined. He was going to make sure Daisy was safe, even if it meant going back across the river.

"It's almost coming over the bridge," Daisy said to Dad.

Dad nodded. "We need to tell them at the farm, fast. Then they can get around in the truck over the other bridge, and make sure everyone's okay." He grinned at Daisy as they followed Baxter off the bridge, through the water again to the path on the other side. "We'd better tell them we've got this little one, as well."

"And that we're keeping him?" Daisy said, hesitantly. Had Mom and Dad really meant it?

But her dad nodded. "And that we're keeping him," he agreed.

Daisy gripped the thick fur under her fingers even tighter. Baxter looked up at her, his ears twitching with relief as they came out of the water at last. Holding his head up high, he set off down the path.

"Look!" Daisy pointed further down the path—lights were coming toward them from the farmhouse. "It must be Julie. They're coming to get us."

Dad hugged her. "We'll have to tell her she's too late, Daisy. We've already been rescued!"

"I still can't believe the river rose that quickly." Julie shook her head. "It's never been that high. We were lucky there were only a few tents close enough to be flooded."

"Did everyone manage to get their stuff out?" Daisy's mom asked.

Julie nodded. "It's all drying

in the stables. And most people are heading home today, like you. I don't think we'll use that end of the field for camping again, though—it could have been so much worse."

Daisy yawned. She'd spent the rest of last night sleeping on Julie's living-room floor, wrapped up in spare blankets. She'd let Oliver have the sofa—she had wanted Baxter next to her, and she didn't want him to get into bad habits. She wasn't going to do anything that might make Mom and Dad angry.

Baxter didn't look tired at all. His eyes were sparkling, and he kept twisting his head around to look at the collar and leash that Julie had given Daisy for him. She said they'd need them when they stopped to let him out on the way home.

Home! She still could hardly believe it. Dad was packing the car now, carefully making a safe space in the back for Baxter. It meant Daisy and Oliver would have a lot of bags around their legs, but they didn't mind.

"I think we're ready," Dad said. "Julie, do you think he has enough room in here?"

Julie looked over. "He should be fine." She smiled at Daisy. "I'm so glad he's going home with you. It's perfect."

Daisy lifted Baxter into the car, gently patting him as she took off his leash. "I can't believe he's really ours," she told Julie, giggling as Baxter licked her cheek. "Not just for the vacation, but forever."

The Lost Puppy

Contents

For Max, and for Georgie Dog

Chapter One
The Best Birthday Present

"Christy! Happy Birthday!" Aunt Nell rushed down the path to hug Christy, with Maisy the dachshund galloping after her.

"Thanks, Aunt Nell!" Christy replied with a smile. "Hey, Maisy, where are the puppies?" she asked. Ever since Maisy had her puppies, she'd been curled up in her pen in the kitchen with them, as though she didn't dare let them out of her sight.

Aunt Nell shook her head. "I think she's getting a bit annoyed with them now that they're so much bigger. They spend all their time climbing over her, and nipping each other's ears, or Maisy's. They can't get over the board we've got across the kitchen door, but their mom can, and she's left them behind to get a break."

"Can we go and see them?" Christy asked. She'd always loved playing with Maisy, but the puppies were even more beautiful than their mom, and she hadn't seen them for a week. She was sure they'd have changed. They were 11 weeks old now, but they still seemed to be growing so fast that she could almost see it happening.

"Puppies!" Christy's three-year-old sister, Anna, demanded, stomping up the path. She loved the puppies as much as Christy did. Christy actually wondered if sometimes Anna thought she *was* a puppy. She curled up in their basket almost every time they came to visit Aunt Nell. Once she'd even tried their puppy food, but luckily she hadn't liked it.

"And hello to you too, Anna." Aunt Nell grinned as Anna hurried past her into the house. Christy chased after her little sister—if she wasn't quick, she'd probably find Anna sitting in the water bowl.

"So are you having a good birthday?" Aunt Nell asked. "Does it feel odd that you've already had your party?" Christy had shared her birthday party with her best friend, Beth, the previous weekend. Beth was two weeks older than Christy, so they'd split the difference.

"No, it's great!" Christy beamed at her. "It feels like I'm having two birthdays!"

"Well, I've got a present for you in the house." Aunt Nell had a curious smile on her face, Christy realized. She started to feel excited about the present.

She looked at her mom and dad, wondering if they knew what it was. Mom had exactly the same expression on her face as Aunt Nell, which Christy supposed wasn't that strange, since they were sisters.

"What is it?" she asked curiously.

"Why don't you come and see the puppies before you open your present?" Aunt Nell suggested. "Otherwise we'll find them all nibbling Anna's toes. It's almost their lunchtime."

The puppies were still having lots of small meals. "Is it oatmeal?" Christy asked hopefully, as they went into the kitchen. The last time they'd visited, the puppies had eaten milky oatmeal, and all of them had dangled their big ears in the bowl—and had come out with oatmeal-crusted ears afterward. It was really funny!

Aunt Nell laughed. "No, sorry, it's just biscuits. Very boring. But they like them. Now that they're old enough for their new homes, I'm weaning them off the milky stuff."

"Are they really big enough to leave Maisy?" Christy asked, peering around the kitchen door at the seething mass of brown and black puppies wriggling around in their pen. Maisy hopped elegantly over the board in the doorway, and headed back to her babies. The puppies saw her coming and flung themselves out of the pen, then scampered across the floor to their mom. Christy giggled. She was sure that she saw Maisy duck her head and dig her paws in as she was hit by a wave of puppies.

Aunt Nell nodded. "A couple of people have come to see them already."

"Six babies," Christy said to Dad, as she crouched down to get closer to the pups. "You always say Anna and I are enough!"

Dad nodded. "Quite enough!"

"I think she'll miss them when they're gone," Aunt Nell said. "But right now I don't think she's going to mind *that* much. And I am keeping one puppy."

"Oh, which one?" Christy asked, crossing her fingers behind her back.

"The little black girl puppy. I'm calling her Maggie. She gets along well with Maisy, I think. And I like that the names both begin with M."

Christy nodded, a little sadly. She had been hoping that Aunt Nell would keep her favorite puppy, the handsome boy with the black back and orange paws. He'd spotted her coming in, and now he trotted over to her eagerly. In her head, she'd named him Lucky, although she hadn't told anyone.

There was no point in naming him, really, since he would be going off to live somewhere else very soon. But Christy hadn't been able to help it. Lucky was just the perfect name for him.

He was such a funny little dog, always bouncing around. Christy rolled a jingly ball across the kitchen floor for him, and he skidded after it eagerly, his paws slipping around on the tiles. He was dashing after it so fast that he overshot, and had to screech to a halt and snatch it out of Maggie's paws. His sister growled at him angrily, then stomped away.

Lucky picked up the ball in his sharp little teeth, and marched triumphantly back to Christy, his ears swinging. Then he dropped it at her feet, wagging his tail and nosing it toward her, asking her to do it again.

Christy stroked his glossy fur. "Oh, you're so beautiful."

Anna, who had been lying on the kitchen floor to be on the same level as the puppies, wriggled her way over to Christy and Lucky, and nuzzled him, nose to nose. Lucky looked slightly shocked, but he nuzzled her, too, and then licked her generously on one cheek.

Anna squealed with delight and was about to lick him back when Mom grabbed her. "No licking the puppies!"

Mom glanced worriedly at Dad, but he was laughing.

"It'll be fine," he told her.

Christy frowned at them. What did

they mean? She was sure Lucky licking Anna just once wouldn't do her any harm.

"Why don't you pick him up?" Aunt Nell suggested. "He won't mind."

Christy gently slipped her hands under Lucky's smooth tummy, and snuggled him against her. He had climbed into her lap before, but she had never actually picked him up. He was so good to cuddle. She sighed quietly as she rubbed her cheek against his warm head, wondering if this was the last time she would see him.

Lucky sighed, too, but happily. He dug his nose under the shoulder of Christy's sweater, which made her giggle and squirm, then he scratched his claws against the fabric lovingly.

Aunt Nell smiled at her. "So, do you like your present?"

Christy looked up, confused.

Dad laughed, and Mom smiled at her, then eyed Lucky meaningfully.

"Lucky? The puppy, I mean?" Christy stared at them all, her mouth falling open in surprise.

"I told you she'd already named him!" Aunt Nell said. "He's always been the one Christy liked best. A lady wanted to choose him yesterday, Christy, but I told her he was reserved for you!"

"You're giving me Lucky for my

birthday?" Christy sounded dazed. "Can we take him home?" she added hopefully. "Or is he mine but at your house?" Mom and Dad had always said no to a dog, because Anna was too young. She looked up at them uncertainly. "You said not while Anna was little...."

"But he's not going to get big enough to knock Anna over," Dad pointed out. Lucky was a miniature dachshund—he'd never be bigger than about a foot tall. "And yes, he's coming home with us. Mom and I have decided you're both old enough now. He'll be yours mostly, Christy, but Anna's allowed to cuddle him, too, okay?"

Christy nodded. She didn't mind sharing at all. She was still shocked that they were actually getting their own dog! "Are we taking him home *today*?" she asked Aunt Nell.

"Absolutely. But you have to eat lunch first. And I made you another birthday cake!"

"Oh, wow! Oh, I have to call Beth and tell her we're really getting a dog!" Christy exclaimed. But then she looked worried. "Don't we need stuff? A basket … and bowls … and … lots of things…."

Aunt Nell held up one finger. "Just a minute." She disappeared into the garage and came back out with a huge cardboard box. "One perfect puppy package. This is your present from me, Christy. Lucky is from your mom and dad, so I said I would give you all the things you'd need to take care of him properly." She put the box down in front of Christy. "It's heavy!"

Lucky wriggled in Christy's arms, curious to see what was in such a huge box. Christy laughed. "I think you and Anna are going to be fighting over it," she told him. "Anna loves boxes." She hugged Lucky gently. It was still hard to believe he was really hers!

Chapter Two
Settling In

Lucky traveled the 20-minute journey to Christy's house in a special cardboard box with flaps and a handle on top, which Aunt Nell had given them. But Mom had said that Christy could get him out as soon as the car pulled up at the house.

When Christy opened the flaps, Lucky was squashed into the corner of the box with his special blanket in his teeth, looking very worried. He really didn't understand what was happening, and he didn't like being jostled around. The box smelled strange, too. He was glad he had the blanket, which smelled of home, and the other puppies, and his mom. But he dropped it when he saw Christy and wagged his tail, just a little. He didn't move out of his corner, though.

"Hey, Lucky...," Christy whispered. "Are you okay? Was it scary being in the car?"

Lucky edged closer to her and stood with his front paws on the side of the box, looking up at her hopefully. He didn't like it in here. He wanted to be petted and held. And fed. He was starving.

Christy laughed as she picked him up and he nibbled at her jacket. "Are you hungry? Aunt Nell didn't want to feed you before we drove home—she said you might get sick. And she thought it would be good to feed you here. Then you'll have good first memories of being with us. In your new home!"

Lucky barked—a sharp, demanding "Feed me!" bark. He was sure he knew what Christy was talking about. Aunt Nell always talked to the puppies. *Should we feed you now, hmm?* That was what she said when she was getting the yummy biscuits out.

"Come on, then!" Christy followed Mom inside, and Dad staggered after them with the huge box, while Anna danced around them, singing a little dog-song she'd made up.

"We need to unpack, and then you'll get your dinner," Christy explained to Lucky, as she put him down gently on the kitchen floor. "Your bowls are in here, and a big bag of the food you like."

But Lucky was distracted from food for a moment, as he looked around the kitchen. Dad quickly closed the door. "We've got to keep him in here for a few days, remember," he told Christy. "Aunt Nell said to get him used to one room first."

"And there are tiles in here," Mom added. "So cleaning up will be easy if he makes any puddles. I know Aunt Nell started house-training him, but he's sure to be a little confused, and he might forget that he needs to go to the bathroom. We'd better put some newspaper down, too, just in case."

Christy carefully unpacked the box, admiring the cute bowls Aunt Nell had bought, with little bones painted on them, and the soft, red padded basket.

"Look! There's a collar and leash!" Christy exclaimed.

"Oh, yes," Dad nodded. "We'll have to get a tag with our phone number on it to put on the collar, just in case Lucky ever gets lost."

Dad held out a big bag. “Here’s the food. Should I open it, Christy? Then you can give him some.”

Christy carefully used the measuring cup to fill the bowl with food—Aunt Nell had explained about measuring out the right amount of puppy chow for Lucky’s size. As she put the bowl down, Lucky immediately stopped sniffing his way along the kitchen cabinets and raced for the food bowl like some sort of trained sniffer dog. He gulped down the morsels in huge mouthfuls, licking all the way around the bowl, just in case he’d missed some. Then he took a long drink of water.

"His tummy's almost touching the ground!" Christy pointed out. It was true. Lucky's little dachshund legs meant he wasn't that high off the ground anyway, and now his stomach looked like a small balloon underneath him. He gave a huge yawn, licked around his mouth again, and then looked for somewhere to collapse and sleep off his enormous snack. He stomped over to his basket, where Christy had put the special blanket that Aunt Nell had given them. She'd explained that it had been in the pen with Maisy and the puppies for the last few days, so that Lucky would have something that smelled familiar.

"Oh, Anna!" Mom sighed.

Lucky's new bed was already occupied. Anna was curled up in the soft basket, fast asleep. Lucky looked at her doubtfully, and then turned to look up at Christy, with his ears perked up just a little in a *Well, what am I supposed to do about this?* sort of way.

Mom gently lifted Anna out of the basket, but Lucky clearly wasn't sure about it now. He stood at Christy's feet, staring up at her pleadingly, and she knelt down next to him. Lucky gave a little sigh of relief and heaved himself onto her lap, circling around her knees a couple of times, and then slumping down in a heap—fast asleep.

Lucky settled into his new home very quickly. And he was growing up, too. He was still small—he was never going to be a big dog—but during the next couple of weeks, he stopped sleeping so much and became more and more adventurous—and a bit naughty. He loved playing in the yard with Christy and Anna, especially digging in the flowerbeds. Then he would trot happily back to the girls, covered in leaves and twigs, and shake himself all over them.

He was also terribly nosy. As soon as he was allowed out of the kitchen, after the first couple of days, he investigated the entire house. Every time Christy wasn't watching he would manage to find himself another secret hiding place, which he would get stuck in. Then he'd howl so she had to come and rescue him. Christy didn't understand how he actually managed to find half the spots, let alone climb into them. When he got trapped behind the washing machine, Dad had to pull it out from the wall for Lucky to escape.

For a dog with such short legs, he was a very good climber, although he was much better at climbing up than down. That never stopped him, though.

About a week after they'd gotten Lucky, Christy let him out into the yard on his own for the first time. Up until now she'd always gone with him, but he needed to go outside to do his business, and she was helping Mom cook.

Christy had just set the oven timer for the chocolate chip cookies they were baking when she realized that Lucky was still outside. She looked out of the kitchen window, but she couldn't see him.

"Maybe he's sitting by the door, waiting to come in," Mom suggested.

But he wasn't. Worried, Christy ran outside, hoping that Lucky hadn't found a gap under the fence. She and Dad had gone all the way around the yard, checking it for holes when they'd first brought him home, but what if they'd missed one?

She raced around the yard, calling anxiously. "Lucky! Lucky!"

Mom stood on the patio, carrying Anna, and peered into the flowerbeds.

Suddenly, Anna laughed and pointed,

and Christy heard a worried little whine somewhere up above her.

"Lucky! How did you get up there?"

He was standing in the doorway of Christy's treehouse, staring down uncertainly. The treehouse had been Christy's birthday present the year before, and it had steps built around the tree trunk. Obviously Lucky had managed to scramble up, but he wasn't so sure about getting down again.

"Oh, Lucky! You aren't supposed to go climbing!"

Dachshunds' long backs meant stairs weren't good for them—Christy was amazed that he had even managed to get up the steps. She reached for Lucky, and he wriggled into her arms gratefully so she could carry him down. Then he ran all around the yard twice, as though he liked the feel of solid ground under his paws.

Getting stuck in the treehouse didn't teach Lucky to be any more cautious, as Christy had hoped it might. He was still only a very little dog, but he seemed to think he was enormous, and he had no fear at all.

A few weeks after they had brought him home, once he had had all his vaccinations and been microchipped, Lucky was ready to go out for his first walk. Christy got out his beautiful blue leash. They were taking Lucky to the park—and she knew he would love it!

"Lucky, keep still!" She was trying to clip the leash on to his collar but Lucky kept wriggling. He'd never worn the leash before, but somehow he knew it meant something exciting.

"Let me check your collar, too...," Christy whispered. Aunt Nell had told her that it was important to fit his collar correctly—not so loose that it would slip off, but not so tight that it would rub. She was supposed to be able to put her finger between Lucky's neck and the collar. "I'll open it up one more hole, because it's a little tight on you. Lucky, stop jumping!" She giggled as he wriggled again and licked her nose.

Christy was a little worried that Lucky would be nervous as they walked to the park—especially with the noisy cars speeding past. But he bounced along happily, sniffing everything they passed. His claws clicked busily on the pavement as he scurried from side to side, occasionally darting behind Christy as he caught another interesting smell. Christy kept having to stop and unwind the leash from around her ankles.

"Are you all right, Christy? Do you want me to take him?" Dad asked.

Mom was walking with Anna,

who was just as much trouble as Lucky, and didn't have a leash, unfortunately.

"No, thank you." Christy shook her head firmly. Lucky was her special responsibility, and she had to be able to take care of him. Surely it couldn't be *that* difficult to go for a walk!

At last they reached the park. It wasn't very far away, but Lucky had probably covered three times the distance by going forward, backward, and sideways, and he was looking a little tired. But as soon as he saw the huge expanse of green grass, and the other dogs racing around, he brightened up immediately, his tail starting to whip from side to side. He sniffed busily at several clumps of grass, and then followed Christy along one of the paths.

"Should we see what he thinks of the ducks?" Dad suggested.

"Knowing Lucky, he'll think that they were put there for him to play with," Mom sighed. But they headed through the park toward the ducks, with Anna running ahead—the ducks were her favorite!

"Oh, watch out, Anna!" Mom called, seeing a man coming down the path with a big German shepherd. Anna loved dogs, and she wanted to pet all of them—even if they looked big and scary, like this one.

Lucky spotted the German shepherd at the same moment as Anna did, and he darted forward, dragging his leash out of Christy's hand.

"Lucky!" Christy squeaked in horror, watching him galloping away.

She looked down at her hand, as though she was still expecting the leash to be in it. Then she raced after him.

Lucky ran up to the huge German shepherd and barked loud, shrill barks at it. He could see Anna next to the bigger dog. She was his, even if she did keep sleeping in his basket. He wasn't going to let some big strange dog scare her. He danced around the huge dog—barking and yapping until he ran out of breath and had to sit down, panting.

The poor German shepherd hadn't even thought of hurting Anna, and was too well-trained to do anything to Lucky, either. She took a confused step backward, toward her owner. She was worried that she might be in trouble, and it was all very unfair.

But her owner patted her. "Good girl, Taffy. Sit. That's a good girl." The man then reached down and picked up Lucky in one hand—while Lucky wriggled and yapped and fought.

Christy came running up. Mom and Dad were chasing after them, too.

"Here you go." The man handed the wriggling puppy to Christy.

"I'm really sorry! It's his first walk—he doesn't really understand other dogs yet...," Christy stammered, hoping the German shepherd's owner wasn't going to shout at her.

"Sorry!" Dad gasped, as he picked up Anna. "I hope he didn't upset your dog."

Lucky was still yapping at the German shepherd, who was now sitting quietly and looking rather smug, as though she knew she was well-behaved and the little yappy dog wasn't.

"It's okay. Just be careful. Not all dogs are as calm as Taffy," her owner told Christy kindly, and he nodded at Dad.

"I won't let him run off again," Christy promised.

"I'm so sorry about that!" Dad said, holding Anna tightly, who was reaching out hopefully as the big dog paced past. "No, Anna, you can't pet her. We shouldn't have let you get so close."

"Let's go home before we get into any more trouble," Mom said, looking around anxiously at all the other dogs in the park.

As the German shepherd and her owner headed off down the path, Christy hugged Lucky tight. He was still staring suspiciously after the bigger dog, his little body tense with anxiety as he twisted in her arms.

"Oh, Lucky!" she whispered. "That dog could have eaten a puppy like you for breakfast!"

"And had room for a couple more," Dad added grimly.

Chapter Three
An Unlucky Accident

"It was so embarrassing," Christy said, blushing as she remembered the disastrous walk the day before. "And then on the way back home there was another big dog—a Labrador—and Lucky barked at him, too!"

Christy had hurried into school that morning to talk to Beth before they went into class. Beth had known they were taking Lucky for his first walk that weekend—Christy had been so excited about it on Friday.

Beth nodded. "I wonder if it's a small dog thing. My grandmother has a Westie named Buster, and he barks at *everything*. Grandma says it's because he knows he's little and he feels like he's got a lot to prove. Lucky might grow out of it," she suggested, a bit doubtfully.

Christy sighed. "Maybe. He's so sweet most of the time—you know he is. But I just couldn't get him to stop barking! Mom called Aunt Nell, and she says we need to take him to obedience classes. So Mom signed him up for some, but they don't start for a few weeks. I don't know what we're going to do until then!"

"I'm sure puppy training will help. He isn't really bad-tempered. Just yappy. He's a beautiful dog, Christy." Beth smiled, remembering. When she'd gone over to Christy's house last week, Lucky had curled up on her lap and fallen asleep. When it was time for Beth to go home, Christy had had to pick him up off her lap still asleep and all dangly, like a stuffed animal.

"Maybe he just needs to get used to other dogs," Christy said. "Or maybe you're right, and he will grow out of it. But I need to make sure I hold on to him really tightly until he does."

Beth frowned thoughtfully. “Couldn’t you take him somewhere quieter for walks for now?” she suggested. “Somewhere with not as many dogs, I mean.”

Christy nodded. “That’s a good idea. I’ll ask Mom and Dad if they can think of anywhere. It’s fall break next week, so we should have more time for walks.” She hugged Beth quickly as the bell rang. “Great idea!”

Christy’s mom liked the idea of a quiet walk. She thought that it would be a fun way to start the fall break, after school on Friday afternoon.

“What about those woods we go past

on the way to your dance class? Maple Grove Park?" she suggested. "People do take their dogs there, but I doubt that many people would be out in the middle of a Friday afternoon."

"That would be great!" Christy agreed.

When they got out of school on Friday, she said good-bye to Beth—who was going to stay at her grandma's place for the week—and rushed to the car, flinging her bag into the back seat.

Lucky was sitting in his new wire travel crate, looking worried. He still wasn't sure about going in the car, and he wasn't really happy about being shut in the crate, but at least he had more space than in the old cardboard carrier.

The woods were only about a 15-minute drive away, and soon Christy was lifting Lucky out, letting him sniff busily at the grass. There were only a couple of other cars there—it looked like the woods would be empty.

It was a beautiful autumn day, really warm for October, and Lucky had a wonderful time racing along with Christy, and flinging himself into piles of dry leaves. They flew everywhere as he rolled and jumped and snapped at them, growling as though he were very fierce. His legs were so short that every so often he disappeared right into a drift of leaves, and then he would come up spluttering and do it all over again.

Christy was laughing so much her tummy hurt. The way Lucky's ears flapped when he jumped made him look like he were trying to take off!

"Oooh, river!" Anna called excitedly, as they came to a little stream running along between deep, sloping banks.

There was an old rickety-looking wooden bridge, and they stood on it throwing sticks in and watching them float past underneath the bridge. Lucky watched them in bewilderment, unsure why anyone would waste good sticks by dropping them in the water. He whined and tugged on the leash, wanting to go and explore some more, and at last they went over the bridge and deeper into the woods.

Christy and Lucky were chasing Anna through the leaves when suddenly Lucky stopped, staring off down the little path they were following. He'd heard something, Christy could tell. He looked as though he were listening with every hair of his body. Then she heard it, too—barking, but much further into the woods. They weren't going to have the place to themselves after all.

"Oh, is it another dog?" Mom said with a sigh. "Hold on to him tightly, Christy. Or I can take him, if you want."

"It's okay, Mom." Christy wound the leash around her hand as Lucky let off a series of earsplitting barks. He jumped around at the end of his leash, wanting to chase after the other dog, but Christy wouldn't let go.

Anna stared at Lucky, wide-eyed. She didn't like it when Lucky barked loudly. She backed away, meaning to grab a hold of Mom's hand, but she wasn't looking where she was going. She tripped over a tree root and fell, scraping the side of her face against the rocky ground.

"Oh, Anna!" Mom came running to scoop her up as she started to howl.

Lucky was so surprised by the noise

Anna was making that he stopped barking. He didn't like loud noises, either—unless he was the one making them. He whimpered and pulled at his leash, trying to get away.

"Christy, can you get the wipes out of my bag?" Mom asked, examining the scrape down the side of Anna's face.

Christy nodded. But Lucky was pulling and tugging at the leash, and she couldn't unzip the bag and hold him at the same time. She looped Lucky's leash over a nearby branch so she could open the bag. "Here they are."

Lucky wriggled anxiously. He didn't like to see Anna upset, and he certainly didn't like the wailing. But once Mom found a couple of pieces of candy in her bag, Anna seemed to cheer up miraculously, and let her wipe the scrape clean. After that, Lucky stopped worrying about Anna and started to investigate the branch that Christy had fastened him to.

He didn't like it. He couldn't move more than half a foot either way without the leash pulling on his collar and hurting his neck. He couldn't go and sniff at that clump of leaves, which smelled as though a couple of other dogs had been there before. He *had* to check that out. And there was a really good, big stick just out of reach that he would love to chew. It wasn't fair! He shook himself impatiently, making the tags on his collar jingle.

"It's all right, Lucky, hang on a minute…," Christy said. But she didn't even look at him—she was still helping Mom with Anna.

Lucky shook himself again, and his leash slipped off the end of the branch and thudded to the ground beside him. He stared at it in surprise. He hadn't meant for that to happen.

If Anna hadn't started to howl again,

because Mom had accidentally wiped her face too hard, Christy would have noticed what had happened and grabbed him. But she was giving Anna a hug to cheer her up.

Lucky eyed them thoughtfully. They were busy. But there was no point in coming out for a walk, and then just sitting on the path the whole time. He padded away, sniffing happily at the leaves. He expected that Christy would come and catch him up in a minute anyway. Another dog had definitely been past—maybe the one he'd heard barking earlier. He would go and find it. He scampered along the path, nose down, following the scent, and leaving Christy and Anna and Mom far behind.

"Is she going to be okay?" Christy

asked Mom worriedly. It looked like a nasty cut, and it was still bleeding, even after Mom had wiped it a couple of times.

"She'll be fine," Mom said. "We need to go home and wash the scrape, though."

"It hurts!" Anna wailed. "An' my fleece! My best fleece!" It was her pink one with the hearts on it, and it was covered with mud all down the side.

"Mom can wash it. It'll be dry by tomorrow, won't it, Mom?" Christy hugged her little sister gently. "Lucky didn't mean to scare you by barking like that. He thought he heard another dog. Didn't you, Lucky?"

Christy turned around to look at him. But Lucky was gone.

Chapter Four
Lucky's Great Escape

The woods were full of birds calling, and squirrels racing up and down the branches. Lucky was so little and so light-footed that on his own, without Mom and the girls, he hardly made any noise at all—only the quiet shushing of his leash, trailing behind him through the leaves. So he saw more of the wildlife than he had before. A robin fluttered from tree to tree—almost as if it were leading him down the path—and Lucky followed, fascinated.

The woods were old, and some of the trees were very large, with odd twisted roots that made little bridges and holes along the path. It was natural for such a small dog to try to wriggle through these rather than going around them, but unfortunately Lucky forgot about his leash. He was hurrying after the robin when he was pulled back with a sudden, horrible jolt. He yelped and turned around, thinking that Christy had caught up with him and grabbed the end of his leash. He looked up angrily. Why hadn't she called him, instead of grabbing him like that? But Christy wasn't there.

Instead, his leash was caught on a root that was sticking out of the ground—really stuck, as he found out when he tried to pull it away like he had earlier. Lucky wriggled, and whined, and whimpered, and pulled, but it was no good. The leash wasn't budging this time.

Lucky sat down, panting wearily. This was just the same as before—he was stuck, when he wanted to explore. He tried pulling again, this time the other way, squirming backward to pull off his collar instead of trying to free the leash.

As usual, Christy had checked Lucky's collar before they set out to make sure there was enough space so it didn't rub him and hurt. But that also meant that if Lucky didn't mind squashing his ears and wriggling very hard, it wasn't actually that difficult to get the collar off.

He burst out of it like a cork from a bottle, rolling over backward and landing in a pile of leaves. He picked himself up and sniffed curiously at his collar and leash. He didn't want to leave them. But he was sure Christy would come along soon, and she could unhook the silly leash for him. He'd let her put it back on him if she'd come and run with him, instead of standing around and spoiling a good walk.

He trotted off through the undergrowth. He'd lost sight of the robin, but now there was an interesting furry, gray creature that was scampering through the branches above him. He wasn't sure what it was, but it bounced and sprang very temptingly, and he was hoping it might come a little lower. He barked at it, but that made it go faster and climb higher, and he had to run to keep up.

"Lucky! Lucky!" came a far-off cry. That was Christy calling him. He stopped for a second, but the squirrel stopped, too, looking down at him so teasingly that he couldn't bear to let it go. He'd try to find Christy in a minute, once he'd caught the squirrel. He set off on a gallop again, and the squirrel leaped through the trees ahead of him.

He was chasing it so desperately that he almost ran into a lady standing in the middle of a clump of bushes, holding a pair of binoculars.

"Shhh!" the lady whispered angrily.

Lucky stopped short, staring at her in surprise. She'd been so quiet that he simply hadn't noticed she was there.

There was a beating of wings and a pair of birds fluttered away, squawking in fright. Lucky watched them go and barked again excitedly.

The lady sighed. "You've scared them away, you silly dog." Then she seemed to realize for the first time that he was all alone. "Where's your owner, hmm?" She looked around, expecting someone to come chasing after him, but the woods were silent. "You don't have a collar! Who do you belong to? They shouldn't be letting you race around here on your own; there's a road close by. Come here.... Here, dog...."

She stretched out a hand to him, but Lucky had heard the irritated tone in her voice after he scared the birds, and now he didn't trust her. He backed away nervously, and as she took a step forward to grab him, he raced off.

He hurried back through the bushes to the path, suddenly wishing that he were with Christy. He'd find her, and then maybe they'd be able to catch the strange furry, gray animal in the trees together. Lucky scurried down the path, expecting at any moment to come to the big trees where he'd lost his leash, and then, a little further, to find Mom and Anna and, most importantly, Christy.

But as he went further and further along, Lucky realized that this might not be the path he wanted. He looked around, and suddenly the trees all seemed so much larger and darker, and different. He had no idea where he was, or where Christy was. He was lost.

"But we can't just leave him!" Christy stared at her mom in horror.

"Christy, we have to go. I'm sorry. We've been searching for a long time." Mom was holding Anna in her arms, who was crying miserably, the scrape on her face still bleeding a little. "I need to get Anna home and clean up her face. It's filthy, and it's been like this for almost an hour."

"If we go home now, we might never find Lucky! Just five more minutes, please, Mom." Christy looked around, desperately hoping Lucky might spring out of the bushes suddenly, and everything would be all right again. But they had searched everywhere, calling and calling. Lucky seemed to have totally disappeared.

"I've called your dad, and he's going to leave work early so you can both come right back and look. I'm really sorry, sweetheart, but we have to get home." Mom set off down the path, carrying Anna.

Christy stood in the middle of the path, looking uncertainly one way and then the other. She couldn't bear the thought of leaving Lucky. Maybe he'd been frightened by something and was hiding. He might come out in just a minute, if they were quiet.

"Christy, please!" Mom called, heading for the bridge over the stream.

Christy trailed after her, trying not to cry. But by the time they reached the car, the tears were streaming down her face.

Lucky padded down another path, sniffing hopefully. He was sure he could smell Christy, but the scent was all over the place. It was very confusing. It didn't help that he was hungry. He wanted to be back at home with Christy, eating his dinner.

Just then, he heard the rushing sound of the stream, and he trotted forward, peering down the steep bank at the water. They had come over the stream, and that had been before Anna had fallen over, he remembered.

He sat down at the top of the bank. Should he cross over again or not? He whimpered miserably, wishing he had run back to Christy when she called him. No. He wouldn't cross over it again. Christy would wait for him where he'd left her, he was sure. By those big trees, where Anna had fallen down. He only had to find them. He turned away from the stream and nosed along, trying to find the path. But so many dogs had walked through the woods that he was distracted and kept losing Christy's scent.

It was starting to get dark, and the woods were gloomy, and full of strange noises, rustlings, and odd bird calls. For the first time, Lucky began to wonder what else might be in the woods, besides that gray creature he'd chased. He wondered if there was anything bigger.

The late afternoon shadows meant that Lucky didn't even notice when he padded over the stream further along its course, where it ran under a fence in a huge metal pipe. Lucky was small enough not to pay much attention to the fence—he simply went under it—and he didn't see the pipe buried in the bank. So he was surprised to find himself almost back at the road.

He came around a corner of the path and pulled up quickly, staring at the wider road at the edge of the path that led into the woods. He knew this place! He was sure of it, even though he hadn't crossed the stream again. This was just a little further from where they had left their car. But the space they had parked in was empty.

They had left without him!

Chapter Five

The Search Party

Lucky sat down on the path miserably. He'd been just about to find Christy, he was sure of it. But it looked like she'd left without him. He couldn't understand why she would go away and leave him. Didn't she want him back? Was she angry because he'd frightened Anna?

He whimpered, staring across the road at the space where the car should have been. Then he whirled around, his tail tucked in, and a tiny growl beginning in his throat.

Behind him was a tall man who'd come jogging down the path, his big white sneakers shining, even in the gathering dusk.

"Hey, it's all right. I almost stepped on you, didn't I, you poor little thing. I'm sorry—I didn't see you there. I was just running, and not really looking." The man crouched down, panting, and stared at Lucky, smiling. "You might just be the smallest dog I've ever seen."

Lucky glared back at him suspiciously, remembering the lady who had scolded him before.

The man held out a gentle hand, and Lucky sniffed at it. The man smelled like another dog, which wasn't good, but aside from that, Lucky felt as though he could trust him. And he didn't know what else to do.

"Who do you belong to? You're not a stray; you're very well taken care of. Beautiful shiny coat, and you're not skinny, even if you are a tiny thing. Where's your collar? I bet you've slipped out of your leash, haven't you? Someone's going to be really worried about you."

Lucky backed away slightly as the man's hand went to his pocket, but all he did was pull out something in a crinkly wrapper and open it. He broke off a piece and held it out to Lucky.

"It's not really the best thing to give a dog, but a little bit won't do you any harm. You try it, pup. It's good. I like them, especially when I've been out for a run. It's an energy bar."

The thing smelled sweet and sugary, and it was making Lucky hungrier than ever. He darted forward and snapped it out of the man's hand, swallowing it in one gulp.

"Nice, isn't it? Want some more? I wonder who you belong to. You must have come here on a walk with your owners, because there are no houses close by, and you're too little to have come far on your own." The man looked around thoughtfully. "So where are they, hmm? I don't want to leave you galloping through the woods on your own, and it's starting to get dark."

He stood up again and looked around. "Hello! Anyone lost a dog?"

The shout echoed through the trees, but no one answered. The only sound now was a light pattering, as it began to rain.

"We're going to get soaked." He looked down at Lucky, who was shivering and pressing himself back against the bushes. "Sorry, pup. Did I scare you, shouting like that?"

He broke off another piece of the energy bar, and this time Lucky nibbled it out of his hand, and let the man pet his head and ears. "Yes, you're a beautiful little boy, aren't you?" He sighed. "What are we going to do with you? There are no cars left, and I can't hear anyone else around. I can't just leave you here on your own. You don't look to me like you've got any road sense at all...."

He stretched out his hand again, and this time Lucky sniffed it eagerly, hoping for more food. But the man picked him up instead, very gently, but firmly enough that Lucky didn't feel as though he was going to be dropped. He snuggled against the man's warm hoodie, feeling a tiny bit better. Of course, the man wasn't the same as Christy, but he was warm, and friendly, and the sugary stuff was very nice.

"Come on, then. You'd better come home with me, while I call the dog shelter." The man tucked Lucky in the crook of his arm and set off down the road.

Lucky stared back at the trees, and the greenish gloomy darkness that was settling between them. He didn't like it here. But what if Christy came back for him and he'd disappeared? He wriggled in the man's arms, and howled. He had to stay and wait for Christy! Surely she was going to come back! And now he wouldn't be there for her!

"Shhh, shhh, I know. But I can't leave you here, pup. Don't worry. We'll find your owners, I promise." The man frowned. "Well, I hope so, anyway...."

On her way back to the woods with Dad, Christy peered anxiously out of the car window. She'd read so many stories about dogs finding their way home that she half-expected to see Lucky trotting down the road toward them.

"Dad!" She pointed to the grassy area. "We parked here, and went up that path." She looked at her watch. It had been an hour since they'd left. She'd had to wait for Dad to get home, and then they'd driven all the way back. Lucky had been missing for two whole hours now.

Her dad parked the car. "Come on, then." He got out, and peered into the darkening woods. "Don't worry, Christy. He's probably just hiding from the rain."

Christy shivered. Somehow the woods looked much less welcoming than they had after school, when the autumn sun had been bright and friendly. But she straightened her shoulders, and marched determinedly up the path, calling for Lucky. He had to be here somewhere.

"Can you remember where Anna fell?" Dad asked, rushing after her. "He might have had the sense to go back to where you left him."

"I think so. It wasn't far from here, just on the other side of the stream." Christy hurried on, crossing over the bridge, and looking anxiously from side to side, calling until her throat started to hurt.

"I can't understand why he isn't coming," she told her dad, stopping at the top of a little slope, and staring around them hopelessly. “I know he’s naughty, but he usually comes if I call him in the yard. He knows I’ll give him treats and cuddle him. Why doesn’t he want to come back to us now?” She leaned against her dad, trying hard not to cry. If she started, she knew it would be hard to stop.

“Christy, don’t worry. This place must be full of amazing smells for a dog.” Dad hugged her. “He’s bound to be off chasing a squirrel or something. And remember what he was like when we met that German shepherd in the park? He might have chased after another dog.”

“We did hear another dog barking.” Christy nodded. “But it sounded like it was a long way away. Dad, he could be *anywhere*," she added. "What if he ran on to the road?" she whispered.

Her dad sighed, and hugged her tighter. "I don't think he'd do that, Christy. He's never tried it before, has he?"

"He's only been on a couple of walks," Christy pointed out miserably. "And if he saw another dog he might."

Her dad shook his head. "There's no reason to think he went on to the road. He's probably sitting under a tree waiting for you. He'll be angry that you left him, knowing Lucky!" Dad was trying to be cheerful, Christy knew, but it wasn't really working.

She kept walking and calling, but still no Lucky, or even an answering bark.

"Hey, what's that?" her dad asked, pointing at a flash of blue among a mass of twisted roots.

"His leash! That's Lucky's leash!" Christy's heart jumped wildly as she scrambled for it, hoping that she might find Lucky curled up fast asleep at the other end. He did sleep very deeply sometimes; he might not have heard them calling.

But all she found on the end of the leash was Lucky's collar.

"Oh, Lucky...," she whispered.

"He must have slipped it off," Dad said grimly. "Well, at least we know he was here. Come on, let's keep looking. We've got about another half-hour before it's completely dark."

Christy swallowed as she looked around at the massive, hulking trees. There were holes and hiding places all over the woods, and it was getting darker by the minute. She was scared, and she was with Dad.

And if she was scared, Christy couldn't help thinking as they hurried deeper into the trees, how frightened must Lucky be, all alone!

Chapter Six
A Strange Night

"I wish I knew what your name was," the man said to Lucky, as he carried him down the road and back toward town. "I suppose I'm going to have to keep calling you pup. I'm Jake, by the way," he added, smiling down at Lucky, who was curled into his elbow, watching everything they passed with anxious eyes. "And we're going back to my place, just for a little while, and then we'll take you to the shelter. Then hopefully your owners will come and find you...."

Lucky glanced up at Jake's face, his ears flattening a little. There was a worried tone to the man's voice again, and he didn't like it.

"Yes, I know. No one would leave you behind on purpose, surely...." He sighed. "Anyway, we're almost home. You're going to meet Mickey." He laughed. "Mickey's going to get a shock when he sees you. I only went out for a quick jog."

He searched in the pockets of his sweatpants for the keys as they came up to a little white house. Lucky leaned forward, listening intently. He could hear the clicking of claws on a hard floor, and a curious snuffling. There was another dog in there! It had to be the one that the man smelled like. He shifted a little nervously in Jake's arms. Usually he barked and barked at other dogs, but then he'd been with Christy. Lucky wanted everyone to know that she was his, and he was taking care of Anna and her.

As the door swung open, a golden-brown head peered slowly around it and stared suspiciously up at Lucky.

"Hey, boy. I've brought a visitor. Don't worry. I don't think he's staying that long." Jake tucked Lucky tightly under his arm, and crouched down to give some attention to his old golden retriever, muttering a stream of reassuring words.

"It's lucky you're such a good boy, Mickey. You're not jealous. The pup's lost, poor little thing. We're going to help him get back home, that's all."

Mickey eyed Lucky thoughtfully, as the dachshund puppy stared back. Then he wagged his long, feathery tail a couple of times, very slowly, and turned around, pacing back toward the kitchen and his cushion.

"You're going to have to be gentle with Mickey," Jake told Lucky. "He's an old gentleman. Twelve years old, and he's a bit lame now. Don't go teasing him!" He put Lucky down, watching carefully to see how he and Mickey were going to get along. Jake knew Mickey was really gentle, but he wasn't used to having other dogs in his house.

Lucky looked around nervously, and then sidled after Jake as he headed into the kitchen, too.

"I know there's a flier from Oakleaf Rescue Shelter here somewhere. I was going to send them some money...," Jake muttered, searching through a pile of papers. "And now I'm sending them a wiener dog instead!" He pulled out a piece of paper covered in photos of dogs. "Ah, good. You two all right?" He looked down at Mickey, now curled up in his basket. Lucky was sniffing thoroughly around the kitchen cupboards, and keeping his distance from the bigger dog. "Okay. Let's call them." He tapped in the number, and then sighed. "I should have known. It's six o'clock already. No one's answering the phone." He put the phone back in its cradle slowly, and stared at Lucky. "Now what do we do with you, pup? We'd better feed you, I suppose. That energy bar won't keep you going for long."

He took a small bowl out of the cupboard and put it down a little way from Mickey's big dog bowl, then poured food into both of them from a huge bag.

Lucky flung himself at it as though he were starving and gulped it down.

"Hopefully senior dog food won't do you any harm this once," Jake said, watching with a smile as Lucky gobbled the dry food. "Let's get you some water, too."

Lucky finished his food and took a long drink of water. Then he watched Mickey, who was still slowly eating his bowlful of food. He edged a little closer, and Mickey turned around and gave him a very meaningful stare. *Don't come near my dinner.*

Lucky wriggled backward on his bottom, and then scuttled under the kitchen table until Mickey had finished and paced back to his bed for an after-dinner snooze.

"You need to be careful, pup," Jake told him, petting his head. "Mickey's a lot bigger than you, and this is his house."

But Lucky was a naturally confident little dog, and he didn't really understand how small he was, either. He was starting to feel a bit more at home now, and he pranced up to Mickey, eyeing the bigger dog with his head to one side.

Mickey stared back, his muzzle resting on the edge of his cushion. He was a beautiful golden color, but his coat was turning silvery now, all around his mouth and eyes. He yawned, showing his very large teeth, and Lucky took a step back again, looking a bit more respectful.

Even the teeth didn't stop him for long, though. Lucky wasn't used to being ignored, and he didn't like it. He padded right up to Mickey and yapped sharply at him.

Mickey laid his ears back. The strange little dog was barking at him now, when he was trying to sleep.

Jake took a few steps closer. He trusted Mickey, but he wasn't taking any chances.

Lucky wagged his tail excitedly and barked again, even louder, wanting to get a reaction out of the bigger dog.

Mickey looked over at Jake, his eyes wide, as if he were saying, *Rescue me from this thing!* But Jake only watched, smiling a little.

Lucky crept closer, head down with his front paws flat against the kitchen floor, yapping and whining, his tail wagging. He was starting to enjoy this now. Maybe the big dog was scared of him!

Mickey huffed out a deep, irritable breath, and stood up, towering over the curious puppy. He put out a massive golden paw, and stood on one of Lucky's too-long dachshund ears.

Lucky wriggled and whined, but Mickey had him pinned. It was a clear message. *This is my house. You do as you're told.*

The puppy rolled over—as far as he could with Mickey holding his ear down—waving his paws in the air to show he gave in, and at last Mickey removed his paw. Lucky stayed on his back, showing off his tummy apologetically, until Mickey sat down in his bed.

Finally, Lucky turned over and wriggled forward, creeping closer to the cushion as Mickey watched him. At the edge of the cushion, the puppy looked up hopefully, and the old dog nuzzled him. With a pleased little squeak, Lucky scurried onto the cushion, and sat down next to Mickey. He did keep glancing up at the big dog, though, to make sure he wasn't about to get the ear treatment again.

Jake laughed. "Taught him his place, have you, Mickey? Can he share your bed for tonight, then?"

Mickey sighed, and slumped down on the cushion, squishing Lucky up against the edge. But the puppy didn't seem to mind. He closed his eyes and snuggled himself up to Mickey's broad back, so he was half-lying on top of the bigger dog—and then the two of them went to sleep.

"Where's Lucky?" Anna asked, as Christy pushed open the kitchen door, the leash dangling from her hand.

Her little sister was sitting at the table with their mom, eating a eating a snack. There was a big white gauze square over her scratched face, but she looked much more cheerful.

Christy gulped, and then turned around and raced upstairs to her bedroom. She couldn't face explaining to Anna. And then she was going to have to tell Aunt Nell that they'd lost her precious puppy, too!

She sat down on her floor, leaning against the warm radiator and sniffing. Lucky liked to snuggle up here, too. He wasn't allowed to sleep in her room, but she carried him up to play sometimes.

Her bedroom door creaked open slowly, and Anna peered around it. "Are you angry?" she whispered.

Christy shook her head. She hadn't thought to be angry with Anna—her little sister hadn't meant to fall over.

"Did Lucky run away cuz I fell over?" Anna said sadly.

Christy put out her arms for Anna to come and hug her. "It wasn't your fault. I should have taken care of him better."

"Oh, Christy! You were helping me take care of Anna." She hadn't seen her mom come in, too. "It was just an unfortunate accident. I'm sure we'll find Lucky. Dad can take you back to the woods really early in the morning."

Christy nodded, but tears were sliding down her cheeks. "He'll be scared out there, Mom. It's so dark—there are streetlights here, but there aren't any out there in the woods! And he'll be cold and hungry." She hugged Anna tighter, and her sister snuggled against her.

"We'll find him tomorrow, Christy, I promise," Mom said.

Christy nodded. But how could Mom promisc that when no one knew where Lucky was?

"Hey, pup!"

Lucky yawned and opened his eyes. Why was Christy waking him up, in the dark?

Then he sat up quickly, looking around in panic. That wasn't Christy!

"Shhh, don't worry. I just thought you might need a quick trip out to the yard before I go to bed. I'm not sure if you're house-trained yet." Jake opened the back door, and the security light came on, sending an orange light into the kitchen, and all of a sudden, Lucky remembered where he was.

Or actually, where he *wasn't*. He wasn't at home in his comfy red basket with Christy asleep upstairs. He was lost.

He whimpered, staring out at the strange, dark yard.

"I know. We'll find your owners tomorrow, hopefully. We'll call the shelter again in the morning." Jake picked him up, and carried him out into the yard. "Go on, then you can go back to sleep."

Lucky wandered out onto the lawn, sniffing the night smell of wet grass. Everything was different, and wrong! Where was Christy? Why hadn't he just stayed and waited for her? Then he would be home by now.

He sat down, raised his head to the sky, and howled.

Chapter Seven

The Search Continues

"What if someone's found him and doesn't know who he belongs to?" Christy said worriedly, looking back at Dad as they hurried into the woods early the next morning. It was chilly, and leaves were whirling in the cold wind.

"He's microchipped, too, remember," Dad pointed out. "If someone takes him to a vet or the dog shelter, they'll be able to scan his microchip, and then they'll call us."

"So why haven't they?" Christy wailed. "Maybe he got stuck down in a badger hole! Aunt Nell said that a long time ago, dachshunds were bred to chase badgers down their holes. Are there badgers in Maple Grove Park, Dad?"

"Probably," Dad admitted. "But I don't think Lucky would chase one…."

"He would!" Christy told him sadly. "He tried to show that German shepherd who was boss, didn't he?"

"Excuse me…," someone behind them called breathlessly.

Christy wheeled around in surprise. She'd been so busy imagining Lucky stuck down a badger's hole that she hadn't seen the lady coming up the path behind them. She hadn't expected anyone else to be here at seven thirty in the morning.

"Have you lost a dog? I'm sorry, I heard you calling…."

"Yes!" Dad replied, and Christy raced up to the lady.

"Have you seen my puppy?" she gasped. "Do you know where he is?"

"A little brown-and-black dachshund? I saw him yesterday—I come here to do birdwatching, you see. I did try to catch him, as I thought he might be lost, but he ran off again."

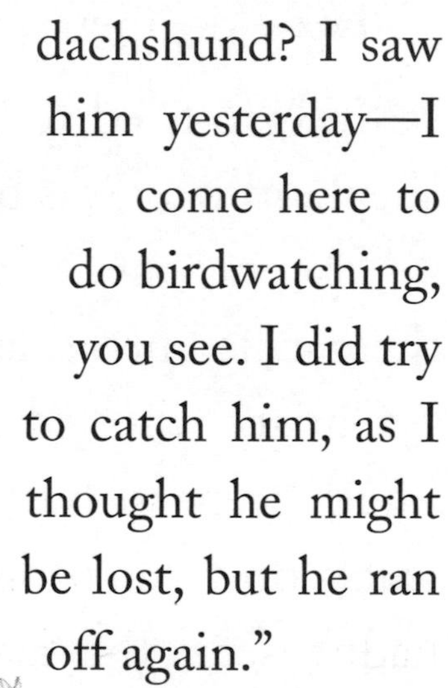

"That's Lucky," Christy whispered. "Did you see which way he went?" she added, rather hopelessly.

"No, but...," the lady paused thoughtfully. "There was a man jogging, and I saw him again as I went back home. He had a little dog with him, and it might have been the same one...."

"Someone took Lucky!" Christy gasped. "He stole him! He must have, or why didn't he call us?"

Dad hugged her. "Don't panic. Lucky slipped out of his collar, remember? Maybe the man took him to the police station. Or the dog shelter in town! That's more likely. We'll go home and call them. Thanks so much," he told the lady. "You've been really helpful."

"I hope you find him," the lady smiled. "He's a sweet little thing."

Christy nodded. She was right—Lucky was so little. Much too little to be out on his own. *He's at the shelter,* she told herself firmly. *He has to be....*

Dad put down the phone, making a face. "Answering machine. But the recorded message says Oakleaf Rescue Shelter opens at nine...."

He checked his watch. Christy had been up at six wanting to go back to Maple Grove Park, and it was still only eight thirty. "It'll take us about 20 minutes to get there," he said thoughtfully.

"Let's go!" Christy grabbed his hand and started pulling him toward the front door.

They sped off in the car, Christy waving to Mom and Anna, who were watching from the door. Anna was really missing Lucky, too. She'd been up almost as early as Christy had, and when Christy and Dad got back from the woods, Christy had found her little sister sitting in Lucky's basket, looking confused and sad.

As they drove through town to the shelter, Christy leaned forward, her fists clenched so tightly her arms ached.

"Relax, Christy," said Dad. "You're not making us go any faster. The shelter doesn't open for another 15 minutes, anyway, and we're almost there."

Christy was out of the car the moment they stopped in the parking lot, and she was off, running toward the doors to the shelter. But it was still locked, and she rattled it uselessly.

"It's only five of nine," Dad called, following her across the parking lot.

Christy paced up and down as they waited outside, checking her watch every 10 seconds or so, certain each time that it must be nine o'clock by now.

At last, they saw a figure coming toward the glass doors, and a young woman smiled at them as she put the key in the lock.

Christy hung on to Dad's arm, as the woman swung the door open. "Good morning!" she said cheerfully. "Have you come to adopt a dog?"

Dad shook his head. "I'm afraid not. We're really hoping that our puppy is here. We lost him yesterday afternoon."

"Oh, I see." The young woman looked doubtful. "I haven't heard about a puppy being brought in." She saw Christy's face fall, and added quickly, "But I wasn't here yesterday, so don't take my word for it. I'll have to check with one of the others. Come on in, anyway."

She led them into the reception area. Christy could hear the noise of barking from down the hallway that led into the main shelter area. She strained her ears, trying to hear Lucky's sharp, dachshund bark. But it was too hard to pick it out. There was a clang of metal, too, which she guessed was the food bowls being put out.

"There's nothing on the computer about a new puppy...." The woman was frowning as she tapped on the keyboard. "Let me go and ask Lucy. She's the manager, and she was in yesterday."

Christy swallowed. It felt like there was a huge lump stuck in her throat, and she was fighting back tears. "Dad, where can he be, if he's not here?" she whispered, choking on her words.

"Don't get ahead of yourself," Dad replied, hugging her. "He might be here." But he didn't sound all that hopeful.

A dark-haired woman came into the

reception area. “Hi, I’m Lucy Barnes. Andrea says you’re looking for a lost puppy? I’m really sorry, but we didn’t havc any dogs brought in yesterday.”

“None at all?” Dad asked worriedly.

“Where can he be, then?” Christy asked, giving up the fight with the tears, and feeling them trickle down her cheeks.

"It may take a couple of days for him to get to us," Lucy explained gently. "Don't give up. Someone may have found him, and they could be holding on to him to see if they can find the owner themselves."

"That man might have stolen him," Christy sobbed. "The lady said she saw a man carrying a dog."

"Let me write down your phone number, and some details about your puppy," Lucy suggested. "Then if someone brings him in to us, we'll get right back to you."

"Thanks. He's a dachshund puppy, 15 weeks old, and he's brown and black," Dad explained, and Lucy typed the details into the computer.

"His name is Lucky," Christy gulped.

"And he went missing yesterday?"

"Yes, from Maple Grove Park. He's microchipped—that should help, shouldn't it?" Dad asked hopefully.

Lucy smiled. "That's great. If he's brought in to the police, or to a vet, they'll call you right away."

"Okay. Well, thanks, Lucy. Come on, Christy." Dad led her out to the parking lot. "I'm sorry, sweetie. Look, we'll stop by the police station on the way back. Maybe he got taken there. And if not, we'll pick up some rolls of tape on the way home, then we can make some posters and put them up on all the lampposts."

Christy nodded, but tears started welling up in her eyes again. If they put up LOST posters, it meant they really had no idea where Lucky was at all.

Chapter Eight

A Happy Reunion

Christy trailed across the parking lot, tears still trickling down her cheeks even though she kept wiping them away. Dad had his arm around her, but it wasn't making her feel any better.

Dad was just unlocking the car when Christy heard someone calling behind them, and running footsteps.

"Wait a minute!" Lucy, the center

manager, was chasing them across the parking lot, looking excited. She spoke into the phone in her hand, "Yes, I've caught them. A brown-and-black dachshund? That's wonderful!"

Christy turned around to look at Lucy, her eyes wide with sudden hope. "Someone's found him!" she whispered.

Lucy nodded at her, smiling hugely as she listened to whoever it was on the other end of the phone.

Christy felt like grabbing the phone. She wanted to know where Lucky was right now!

Finally Lucy ended the call, and grinned at Christy and Dad. "36 Elm Lane. A very nice-sounding man named Jake Harper went jogging in Maple Grove Park last night, and found a little brown-and-black dachshund puppy with no collar or leash. He called us, but we were closed, so he tried again just now to ask if it was okay to bring the puppy in." Her grin got even bigger. "I told him we'd save him the trouble and send you there instead! I hope you don't mind...."

"Thank you!" Christy flung her arms around Lucy and hugged her tightly. "Oh, that's the best news!" She let go and looked up at Lucy worriedly. "It has to be Lucky, hasn't it?" she asked. "There couldn't be another dachshund in the woods...."

"Jake was sure it was your puppy. The age sounded about right, and dachshunds aren't that common. Now go and get him!"

Dad smiled at Lucy. "Elm Lane, right? Thanks for all your help. Come on, Christy!"

"'Bye!" Christy jumped into the car, fighting with her seat belt. She was suddenly so nervous that her fingers seemed to have stopped working. It had to be Lucky, it just had to. She couldn't bear to be disappointed again.

Lucky was lying in the middle of the cushion, with his head on his paws, watching as Mickey ate his breakfast.

It was dog food from a tin this time—different than the food Lucky had at home. He liked the smell, but somehow he wasn't very hungry, even though there was also a big helping for him.

"You're quiet this morning." Jake crouched down by the basket. "I hope you're not sick. Especially since I think I've found your owner. A young lady's very worried about you, apparently. Maybe you're just missing her, mmm?" He stood up. "Well, it won't hurt you to miss one breakfast, I suppose, if you don't feel like it. Do you want to go outside? Quick sniff around the yard? No?" He patted Lucky's smooth head. "Not long now, pup. Cheer up."

Lucky had lifted his head to look at Jake while he was talking, but now that the big man was walking away, he let it flop back down. He didn't want food, and he didn't want to go out in the yard. He wanted Christy.

He wanted Christy pouring out his dog food, and watching him lovingly while he wolfed it down. He wanted to race up and down the yard with her and Anna. He liked Jake, and Mickey was good to share a bed with for one night. But he didn't want to stay here.

He'd never really known another dog before. Especially not one that stood on his ears! This was Mickey's house, and Jake was Mickey's special person. Mickey had made that very clear, and Lucky didn't mind. He just wanted to be back home with Christy.

Elm Lane wasn't far from the shelter, and Christy and her dad pulled up outside number 36 about 10 minutes later.

They could hear barking from inside, even before they rang the bell, and Christy looked up at Dad with shining eyes. It was a squeaky sort of bark. A bossy little dog's bark....

"It's him, isn't it?" Christy whispered,

and Dad nodded, beaming.

On the other side of the door, Lucky scratched and yelped, clawing at the wood panels. He could hear Christy! She'd come to find him!

As the door opened, a small brown-and-black ball of fur hurled itself at Christy, barking and yapping.

She picked him up, laughing and crying at the same time. "Lucky! Where did you go? We looked everywhere for you! Oh, I missed you!"

Lucky licked her face lovingly, then went back to jumping and wriggling, and wagging his tail so hard his whole back end wagged, too. He leaned dangerously far out of Christy's arms to lick Dad, too, and even licked Jake.

Jake laughed. "Yes, you're happy now, aren't you, pup?"

"Thank you for finding him," Christy said shyly, so quietly that Jake could hardly hear her over the loud barking.

"That's all right. He didn't have a collar. I guess he must have lost it."

"He was wearing one." Christy nodded. "My little sister, Anna, fell over a tree root, and I was helping Mom cheer her up. I hooked Lucky's leash over a branch, and by the time we'd calmed Anna down, he was just gone!" Her voice squeaked with fright as she remembered it. "I bet you went off chasing squirrels, didn't you?" she asked Lucky. "The woods were full of them."

Then her eyes widened, as Mickey lumbered into the hallway to see what was going on. "Oh! You've got a dog, too." She looked worriedly up at Dad, and then at Jake. "I'm really sorry if Lucky fought with him. . . ."

Jake laughed. "Actually, he tried being a bit bossy, but Mickey stood on him. After that he was very good!"

"Stood on him?" Christy gasped, looking at Mickey. He was huge.

He looked like he could squash Lucky.

"Just on one ear, just for a moment. His way of showing Lucky who was in charge, I think. Has he been difficult with other dogs before, then?"

Christy shuddered. "He barks at them. It's like he thinks he's as big as they are." She looked down at Lucky, who'd wriggled out of her arms and was dancing around Mickey's legs, nuzzling him playfully. "But he's being so nice to your dog now!"

Jake grinned. “Maybe he just needed a lesson on who’s in charge of the pack. Have you tried puppy parties?”

Dad shook his head. “I haven’t even heard of them. Is it like training? We’re registered for a class that starts in a couple of weeks.”

“Oh, well, the people running your training might do puppy parties, too—you should ask. It’s like a safe place for young dogs to get to know each other. It teaches them how to get along, and figure out who’s in charge. But you’re there to step in if there are any problems.”

“You know a lot about dogs,” Christy said wistfully. She wished she knew as much. She felt like she’d let Lucky down so badly, losing him in the woods, even if Mom had said it wasn’t her fault.

Jake smiled at her. "He really missed you, you know. Mickey distracted him last night, but when I woke him up to go outside to do his business before I went to bed, he seemed miserable. And this morning, he just sat in the basket looking lonely—didn't even want any breakfast. He didn't want me, even if I have been a dog-owner for years. He's your puppy."

Christy nodded, watching as Lucky wove in and out of Mickey's legs. Then he stopped suddenly, looking around, as if he were checking that Christy was still there.

She crouched down, and he raced over to lick her hand quickly before going back to his game.

"See?" Jake nodded at Christy. "Your dog."

Christy smiled. It was true. And she was going to make sure she never lost him again.

Dad had called home to let Mom and Anna know that they'd found Lucky, so Christy wasn't that surprised to find Anna in the front yard waiting for them. She was standing on the bottom of the gate, peering over the top, and she waved madly as soon as she saw the car.

For once, Dad had let Christy hold Lucky on her lap instead of putting him in his travel crate. Every so often, as they drove along, he turned and looked up at her, as though to check that she was still there, and he kept giving her hands loving little licks.

"Lucky, Lucky!" Anna flung open the gate, and rushed over to them, with Mom chasing after her.

"Oh, Christy, I'm so glad you've got him back," Mom said, smiling through the car window.

Christy got out of the car, and Lucky licked Anna, very gently. He could see that the white patch on her face meant he had to be careful.

"Good boy," Christy whispered. She went in through the gate, expecting Lucky to jump down and race around the yard, like he usually did. But this time he stayed snuggled in Christy's arms.

There was nowhere else he would rather be.

Leo All Alone

Contents

For Alice, Max, and Georgie

Chapter One
Puppies for Sale

"Evie, did you put these in the shopping cart?" Evie's mom was staring at a packet of rice cakes, looking confused.

"No. Why would I, Mom? They look horrible." Evie made a face. "It was you, don't you remember? You said they might be nice to nibble on when you were feeling sick. But I bet they'll just make you feel even more sick."

Her mom sighed. "You're probably right." She smiled apologetically at the cashier, who was waiting for them to pay. "Sorry. I seem to be a bit forgetful at the moment."

The girl smiled back. "That's okay. My sister's pregnant and she locked herself out of the house twice last week. How long until the baby's due?"

"Another nine weeks." Evie's mom sighed again. "The time just seems to be creeping by at the moment." She patted her enormous tummy.

"Mom, can I go and look at the bulletin board?" Evie asked. She was getting bored with baby talk. Ever since her mom's bump had begun to show, complete strangers had started talking to them in the street, asking about the baby. They always asked Evie how she felt about having a little brother or sister, and she was sick of having to smile and say she was looking forward to it. She was, but the attention was starting to get on her nerves. And she had a horrible feeling that it would get a lot worse after the baby arrived.

"Of course you can. Actually, Evie, see if anyone's selling any baby stuff. It would be a good way to find some bargains."

Evie sighed quietly. Honestly, did Mom ever think about anything else? She wandered over to the big board behind the Customer Service desk where they put up the advertisements. You could find some really fun things sometimes.

Once she'd spotted an advertisement for a pair of almost-new roller blades that someone had grown out of. She'd been able to afford them with her own money, and they were great.

She browsed through vacuum cleaners, lawn mowers, a girl offering to babysit—and then caught her breath in delight. The next ad was larger than some of the others, and it had a photo attached—a basket of the cutest little white puppies, all climbing over each other. One of them was grinning out at Evie, a naughty glint in his eye.

WESTIE PUPPIES READY FOR HOMES NOW
REASONABLE PRICE
Call Mrs. Wilson at 555-2961

Evie sighed adoringly. That puppy was beautiful! She had to show him to Mom. She looked back over at the line to see if she was done yet. Her mom was looking around for her, and Evie waved, and then dashed over.

"Come and see! You'll love it. Anyway, you shouldn't be pushing that on your own, Mom. Dad would be really angry." Evie helped her mom with the cart, giving her a stern glare.

"Dad worries too much," Mom chuckled. "What am I looking at?" She stared at the board, trying to figure out what Evie was so excited about. "We're not buying a trampoline, Evie," she said, grinning. "And we definitely don't want a speedboat!"

"No, look, I just wanted you to see this cute photo." Evie pointed out the basket of puppies. "Aren't they sweet?"

"Oh, yes, they're beautiful. What kind of dog are they? Westies...." Mom gazed thoughtfully at the photo. "Westies are small dogs, aren't they?" she mused quietly.

Evie nodded. "I think Mrs. Jackson down the road has a Westie. You know, Tyson? He's so cute."

"Mmmm." Evie's mom nodded. "Okay. I suppose you're going to insist on pushing this shopping cart now, aren't you? Actually, Evie, do you want to go and look at the animal magazines? I have to go to the restroom again." She sighed theatrically. "Stay by the magazines. I'll only be a minute."

As soon as Evie set off, her mom searched hastily in her purse for a pen. Then she made a note of the name and phone number from the puppy advertisement on her receipt, and hurried after Evie.

As they drove home, Evie gazed out of the window, daydreaming about puppies. She had no idea that her mom was sneaking glances at her every so often. Over the last few weeks, Evie's mom and dad had been worrying about how the new baby was going to affect her. After all, eight was quite old to suddenly have a new baby brother or sister. Evie seemed to be happy about it, but it was difficult to tell. They'd been wondering what they could do to keep her from feeling left out, and it was only the day before that Evie's dad had thought of getting her a puppy. Her mom hadn't been too sure.

"Won't it be a lot of hassle, just before the baby comes?" she'd worried.

"We've got a few weeks. And the point is that Evie would be taking care of the puppy. It'll give her something to fuss over when we're fussing over the baby." Evie's dad was really enthusiastic. He liked dogs, and he knew Evie would love a puppy. After all, a puppy had been at the top of her Christmas list for the last three years. Her parents had always said she wasn't quite old enough—mostly because Evie's mom thought having a dog would be a lot of work. But Evie's dad had been trying hard to convince her, so the Westie ad had turned up at the perfect time.

"What are you thinking about, Evie?" Mom asked her, smiling. "You're miles away."

Evie grinned. "Just that adorable puppy. I know we can't have one, but if we did, I'd like one just like him...."

Evie's dad got home just in time to help make dinner, and Evie told him about the little white dog as she was setting the table.

"Puppies? For sale now?" he asked thoughtfully.

Evie saw him exchange a glance with her mom and caught her breath, her eyes widening in sudden hope. She looked back and forth between them. Her dad was grinning. "Funny that you saw that ad today, Evie. Your mom and I were talking last night. We've been thinking about getting you a dog, and now seems to be the right time."

Evie could hardly believe her ears.

"You mean it?" she breathed delightedly.

Mom nodded. “If you think you can take care of a dog properly. It’s a big responsibility.”

Evie nodded so hard that she made her neck ache. “I know, I know. I can!”

Mom smiled. “So, shall I call the lady with those puppies? You’d like a Westie?”

Evie just gaped at them. She’d wanted a dog for so long, and her parents had always said, “Maybe,” and “Perhaps when you’re older.” Then she suddenly realized what her mom had just said and squeaked, “Yes! Yes, please!”

Evie hardly ate any dinner. She watched her parents, eating impatiently, and when her dad had swallowed his last mouthful of pasta, she snatched the plate away to put in the dishwasher.

"Hey! Evie! I was going to have seconds!" He smiled. "Okay, okay. Let's put you out of your misery."

Evie waited anxiously while her mom called the number. What if all the puppies were gone? After all, they didn't know how long the advertisement had been up there. She sat on the stair listening to her mom. It was hard to tell what was going on, but eventually her mom said, "Great. Well, we'll come around tomorrow morning. Thanks!" and then she put the phone down and beamed at Evie.

"I'm getting a puppy!" Evie gasped, jumping up and down in excitement. "I can't believe it! I have to go over and tell Grandma!"

Evie's grandma lived a couple of

streets away with her own two dogs, Ben the Spaniel, and Tigger, who was a Greyhound cross with crazy stripes. Evie heard them barking madly as she rang the doorbell. She grinned to herself. She couldn't wait to introduce Ben and Tigger to her new puppy!

"Guess what, guess what!" she announced as Grandma opened the door. "I'm getting a dog!" She didn't manage to say much after that as Tigger was jumping up and trying to lick her face.

"Down, Tigger! Stop it, silly boy. It's only Evie; you see her every day!" Grandma shooed the dogs away and went into the kitchen to put the kettle on. "Darling, did you say you were getting a dog?"

"A puppy! Mom and Dad are giving me a puppy—we're going to pick one out tomorrow morning." Evie sighed blissfully.

Grandma looked confused. "But … just before the baby arrives?"

Evie nodded happily. Then she leaned over the table, lowering her voice as though she were telling secrets. "They didn't say, but I think it's to make me feel better about the baby," she explained.

Her grandma nodded thoughtfully. "Well, everyone would understand if you found it difficult, Evie, you know that, don't you?"

"Grandma, you know I'm really looking forward to it." Evie laughed. "And now I'll have a puppy, too!" She beamed at Grandma, expecting her to be really excited. But Grandma was stirring her tea thoughtfully. "What's the matter?" Evie asked, frowning.

"Nothing, Evie. It's wonderful news. It's just…." Grandma sipped her tea. "I'm just wondering if this is the right time. With the baby coming. A new puppy will be a lot of work, you know."

Evie shook her head. "Don't worry. I know about taking care of dogs from helping with Ben and Tigger, and Dad knows a lot about them, too." Evie bent down to scratch Tigger behind his ears, so she didn't see her grandma's worried face. "I've wanted a dog for so long! I still can't believe it's really happening!"

Chapter Two
Leo's New Home

Evie just couldn't stay in bed the next morning. She usually loved sleeping in on Saturdays after getting up for school all week, but today she was much too excited. She hardly ate any breakfast, either—she just stirred her chocolate cereal in circles until it looked like mud.

"You might as well eat it, you know,

Evie," her mom pointed out, slowly buttering a piece of toast. "We're not going yet. I told Mrs. Wilson we'd be there at 10."

"But that's hours away!" Evie wailed.

"Mrs. Wilson has to feed the puppies and get everything ready," her mom explained. "We can't go over there before then."

"I suppose," Evie agreed reluctantly. She trailed upstairs, wondering what she was going to do to fill an entire hour before they could leave. Then she had an idea. She'd go and look up puppies on the internet to try and find out about taking care of a dog. Evie settled down at the computer and before long was busy making notes. By the time her mom called her downstairs, Evie's head was bursting with information about feeding, walking, vaccinations, and training. It was a lot to think about. But she knew she could do it!

"Oh, look! He's all shy!" Evie giggled, and stretched out her hand to the fluffy white puppy who was peeking out at her around his mother. He took a step back, then curiosity got the better of him. Tail slowly wagging, he began to sneak forward to where Evie was sitting on the floor.

"He's a little cutie, that one, probably my favorite," Mrs. Wilson said fondly. "I'm going to miss him—he's such a sweet-natured dog."

Mom shook her head. “I don’t know how you can bear to see them go. They’re all so beautiful.” She scratched the puppy she was cuddling under the chin, and the little dog snuffled happily at her fingers.

"Well, this is the last time I'll have to, actually." Mrs. Wilson sighed. "Lady and I are getting too old for puppies! We're retiring, aren't we, my special girl?" She patted the puppies' mother, a beautiful snow-white dog with melting brown eyes. "We're going to live by the sea. Lady loves walking along the beach. And getting soaking wet!"

Evie could have sworn that Lady's eyes sparkled naughtily. That was the amazing thing about her and the puppies—they all seemed so bright and intelligent. Then the fluffy little boy puppy suddenly nuzzled at her hand, and she squeaked in delight. She'd been watching Lady and hadn't noticed him creeping up on her.

"He seems to have taken a liking to

you, Evie." Dad laughed, watching the puppy chasing Evie's fingers as she danced her hand up and down.

Evie nodded, and then looked seriously at both Mom and Dad. "Is it really up to me to choose?" she asked worriedly. "I mean, all four of them are wonderful."

"It's a hard job," Dad agreed. "But we can't take them all."

Evie giggled as the little boy puppy scrambled up her jeans, trying to climb into her lap. She helped him out with a boost under his little back paws, and he heaved himself up. Then he turned around four times, gave a great sigh of satisfaction, and went to sleep curled up tight in a little white ball.

Evie looked up, her eyes glowing. "This one," she said firmly.

"Mmm, I don't think you had much choice," Dad agreed, smiling. "He's definitely chosen you! Now you just have to think of a name for him."

Evie smiled. "I know what I'm going to call him. His name is Leo."

Mom and Dad gazed at the little puppy. "That's a perfect name," said Mom. "He looks just like a Leo."

It was so difficult to leave Leo behind, but Evie knew she'd see him again the next day. He'd be coming home with them! Now they just had to get everything they needed to take care of him. Mrs. Wilson had given them a list, and Evie studied it in the car on the way to the pet store.

"Basket. Food bowl. Water bowl. Collar. Leash. Harness. Chew toys," she muttered.

Dad sighed. "Nearly as bad as the baby," he moaned. "You sure little Leo doesn't need a bassinet as well, Evie?"

It was so exciting later that afternoon to see the basket with its bright red cushion waiting in a warm spot in the kitchen, and the collar and leash hanging from one of the hooks in the hallway. Everything was ready for Leo to come home.

"Oh, look! He's found his new basket!"

Evie and her parents were watching Leo explore his new home. He was trotting around on unsteady paws, sniffing at everything.

"Ah-choo!" Leo sneezed and stepped back, shaking his head.

"Oops!" said Dad. "I didn't know my boots smelled that bad. Let's leave him to settle in."

That night, Evie sneaked back down to the kitchen after her bedtime to check that Leo was okay. He'd eaten all his dinner and seemed to have made himself at home, but she was worried that he would be lonely, since he was used to sleeping with his mom and his brother and sisters. Leo had been lying awake. He'd been trying to make sense of all the strange things that had been happening that day. His first car ride; the new house; a new basket to sleep in.

And new people. They seemed very nice —the girl smelled friendly, which was important.

The door clicked open softly, and Leo's ears pricked up. It was the girl, Evie. "Shhh!" she whispered. "We can't let Mom and Dad hear us, Leo. You're supposed to stay in your basket, but I bet you're scared down here on your own. I'm taking you up to my bedroom instead. Mrs. Wilson said you were very well house-trained, so I'll put some newspaper down for you, okay? Mom would be upset if you peed on my rug!" She snuggled him close as they crept up the stairs, and Leo settled into her arms. This was much better than a basket, even a nice one like he'd been given.

Of course, Evie's mom and dad soon figured out exactly what was going on, but they were so glad that Leo was settling in, and making Evie so happy, that they pretended not to notice. From that night on, Leo slept on Evie's bed every night, snoring gently.

It didn't take long for Leo to become part of the family. He was such a friendly little dog. After a couple of weeks, when he'd had all his shots, he was allowed to go out for walks, which meant he could go to school to pick up Evie. She loved coming out to see Mom waiting with Leo on his bright red leash. Usually it was twisted all around his paws and he tripped over it as he tried to race over to her. Her friends were all really jealous, and Leo got petted by everyone. Then they'd head home and Leo would watch TV with Evie on the sofa. He soon decided on his favorite programs, and he got very good at singing along to the theme songs in a howl.

Mom hadn't been so sure about getting a dog, but Leo won her over very quickly. He loved people, and he followed her around the house as she did the housework. He was much better company than the radio! And whenever she sat down, he rested his head on her feet.

Of course, Leo didn't have to work hard to charm Evie's grandma. She was always popping over to see him and Evie, and it was great to have her to ask about dog-training tips. It only took

Leo a few days to learn about asking to go outside and Grandma warned Evie not to give him too many doggy treats as a reward, as he was starting to look a little chubby!

Once Leo could meet up with other dogs, Evie took him over to Grandma's house to be introduced to Ben and Tigger. Leo was a little shy at first—they were a lot bigger than he was, especially Tigger—but after half an hour he was chasing them around the yard. Ben the Spaniel soon figured out a good way to calm Leo down when he was being too excitable—he sat on him! Evie panicked the first time he did it, but Grandma said it would probably be good for Leo to have an older dog bossing him around, and that Ben wouldn't hurt him.

Evie and Dad soon got into the habit of taking Leo for an evening walk after dinner. It gave Mom the chance to snooze on the sofa in front of the television. Now that the baby was getting really big, she was tired a lot of the time. Dad and Evie always took a ball with them, or Leo's favorite, a rubber disk. Dad had seen it in the pet store and bought it for when Leo was bigger, but once Leo saw it, he didn't want to wait. So what if the disk was almost as big as he was? He was very good at catching it—he could do massive leaps in midair, twisting and turning and snatching the disk as it fell. Then he'd haul it over the grass back to Evie, and sit panting exhaustedly for a minute, before yapping for them to throw it again. A couple of times he'd worn himself out so much that Dad had to carry him home and lay the exhausted puppy in his basket. Evie was so happy that Leo had become part of the family —she couldn't imagine life at home without him now.

Chapter Three

A New Arrival

One night, Leo was curled up snugly in a nest of comforter on top of Evie's toes. He was twitching happily in his sleep, dreaming of breakfast, when he was woken by the sound of Evie's parents talking. He sat up and listened carefully—it wasn't something he expected to hear in the middle of the night. Something interesting was going on. He padded up to the top of the bed, and licked Evie's ear.

"Grrmmpf!" Evie wriggled and wiped the drool off her face. "Leo! It's the middle of the night, silly. What are you doing?" She yawned, and gave a little stretch. "Go back to sleep. It's a long time until we have to get up." Then she turned over and snuggled her face back into her pillow.

Leo huffed through his nose irritably. Why wouldn't Evie listen? Couldn't she tell that something exciting was happening? He grabbed Evie's pajama sleeve with his teeth, very, very gently, and pulled.

"Okay, Leo, what is it?" she asked sleepily. "Do you need to go to the bathroom? Because if you think I'm taking you all around the yard to find a good place at this time of night you can think again!"

Leo yapped sharply, and tugged at Evie's sleeve again. Then he dropped the sleeve and stood silently, his ears pricked up.

Evie listened, and at last she understood why Leo was behaving so strangely. Her parents weren't just talking now, they were moving around, too. Doors were opening and shutting quietly, and she could hear her dad on the phone to someone, sounding anxious. The baby was coming! It had to be that. Evie pulled her pillow up and leaned back against it, whispering to Leo to come and sit with her. He burrowed in under her arm and they listened together in the dark. Someone was arriving downstairs.

"That'll be Grandma, I bet," Evie whispered. "They said they'd ask her to come and stay with me when they had to go to the hospital."

Leo grunted in agreement. He liked

Grandma. She had dog treats in her purse.

A few minutes later, the front door banged, and they heard someone coming back up the stairs. At last Evie's bedroom door eased open, and Grandma poked her head around.

"Hi, Grandma!" Evie whispered.

"Hello, darling! I thought you might have woken up, with all the coming and going. I just came to check on you."

"Leo woke me up. Is Mom having the baby now?" Evie sounded anxious.

Grandma perched herself on the end of Evie's bed, and petted Leo's nose.

"Clever Leo. Yes, they think so. Don't get too excited, though—these things can take a while." She smiled down at Evie, still cuddling the little dog, and decided that she'd been wrong to worry. Evie loved him so much, and a dog would be just what her granddaughter needed to keep her company over the next few weeks.

The next day Evic's parents brought baby Sam home. Evie's mom and Sam were both doing really well, and they didn't need to stay in the hospital. Mom said the noise of all the other babies in the hospital was driving her insanc, and she wanted to be home in her own bed.

Even though they wcre coming home as soon as they possibly could, the wait still seemed like forever to Evie. It was a Saturday, so shc was home, with Leo and Grandma. The day really dragged, even though as a treat they all walked to a nearby restaurant to get lunch. Grandma stood outside with Leo, who was blissfully breathing in the smell of fries, and Evie went in to get their food. When they got back, both Evie and Grandma naughtily fed Leo the odd fry under the table, so he was soon full and fast asleep.

Evie couldn't help listening for the car—Dad had called to say they'd be home sometime that afternoon, and they just had to wait for the doctor to give Mom one last check. Their road was pretty quiet, but Evie ran to the window to look at least ten times before she finally spotted their car pulling up.

"They're here!" she squeaked. Grandma came hurrying over to join Evie.

Evie's dad was trying to get the new baby seat out of the car and all they could see of her new brother was a little bit of blue blanket trailing out of the seat.

Leo couldn't tell what Evie was thinking, which was odd, because usually he had a good idea. Was she happy about this strange new thing that was happening? He licked her hand, and made a questioning little "wuff?" noise.

"That's the baby, Leo. My brother, Sam. Let's go and see." Evie scrambled down from the windowsill, and Leo trotted after her out into the hallway. Grandma had opened the door, and Evie's parents were just bringing the baby in.

"Evie!" Mom hugged her tightly.

"I missed you. Were you and Grandma okay?"

"Of course. Can I see him, Mom?" Evie crouched down next to the baby seat and peered in. Sam seemed tiny inside—just a small hand clenched tightly around the blanket, and a pale little face half-covered by a hat.

"Let's get him in and unwrap him, then you can see him. It's a little chilly outside so he had to be covered up," Mom explained.

Leo followed interestedly as the family went into the kitchen. The baby smelled new and different, and he wanted to investigate.

Grandma and Evie watched as Mom unzipped Sam's little jacket, with Dad's help. At last she stood up, and carried him over. “Do you want to sit down, Evie?” she asked. “Then you can hold him.”

Evie whisked over to a chair and sat down, eagerly holding out her arms.

Mom kissed Sam’s nose, and handed him very carefully to Evie. “Sam, this is your big sister!”

Evie sat holding Sam, a look of amazement on her face. “He’s smaller than some of my old dolls,” she whispered, looking worriedly up at Mom. “Is he all right?”

Dad laughed. “He’ll grow. You were smaller than that.”

Evie gazed down at Sam, watching as his eyes gradually opened. “He’s looking right at me!” she squealed, beaming in delight.

Mom laughed. "I think he is! They say new babies can't really see much, but he's definitely staring at you."

"You know, he looks a lot like Evie," Dad put in.

"Yes, I see what you mean," Grandma agreed.

Leo watched as they all chattered excitedly. He was feeling confused. No one had introduced him to the new baby. Evie was his person, and she was ignoring him. He gave a sharp little yap, and everyone jumped. The tiny creature on Evie's lap gasped and let out a shuddering wail that made Leo back away. What was it?

"Leo!" Evie said angrily. "What did you do that for? Look, you've made Sam cry."

Leo backed away even further, his tail tucked between his legs. Now Evie was angry with him. He wasn't sure he liked this *baby* thing at all.

Over the next few days, Evie fell in love with her new little brother. Sam didn't do much, except lie in a bassinet and wail occasionally, but he was very cute. Evie's dad had some time off work to help out, so Evie had tried arguing that she ought to have time off from school, too, but apparently it didn't work that way. She had to go back to school on Monday morning. Dad dropped her off in the car.

"You will bring Sam to pick me up, won't you?" she begged her mom. "I want everyone to see him. He's so much nicer than anyone else's little brothers and sisters."

The trip to pick up Evie from school was the first time Mom had taken Sam out in his new stroller. Leo watched as Dad wrestled with the stroller. It would be nice to take a walk. He'd been let out in the yard over the weekend, but no one had taken him for a proper run, and he was anxious to be out smelling some good smells. Leo went to fetch his leash—it hung over a hook in the hall, and he could tug it down. He trotted back with it in his mouth just as Mom was maneuvering the stroller over the front step.

"You're sure you don't want me to come?" Dad asked again.

"No, you start making the tea; we'll be fine." And she closed the door behind her. Without Leo!

Leo barked to remind Mom she'd left him behind—it wasn't like her to forget, but maybe that baby had distracted her.

"Not today, Leo." Dad shook his head. "Sorry, boy, but it's a bit much to have you *and* the stroller." He patted Leo's head and went back into the kitchen, leaving Leo in the hall, his leash still trailing out of his mouth.

Leo stared at the door, confused. He always went to pick Evie up from school. Was Evie's mom really not coming back for him?

"Leo! Treat!"

Evie's dad was calling. Leo gave the door one last hopeful look. Oh, well. He supposed a treat was better than nothing....

When Mom and Evie got back from school, they were both looking a bit frazzled. Sam had snoozed most of the way, and then woken up just in time for everyone to say how cute he was, but now he was hungry, and upset, and a loud wailing noise was coming from his nest of blankets.

Mom sat on the sofa to feed him, and Evie curled up next to her to watch —she'd really missed seeing Sam while she was at school. Leo jumped up, too —he thought they were going to watch television together, like they usually did. But Evie squeaked in horror and pushed him off. "Leo, no! You might squash Sam!"

Leo's tail drooped, and he slunk miserably into the kitchen. The baby was going to watch all his favorite shows with Evie instead. It wasn't fair.

All the next week, people kept stopping by with presents for the new baby, and quite often one for Evie, too. Everyone seemed to think Sam was very special, and he got fussed over all the time. Leo wasn't quite sure why. Sam didn't do a lot, and he certainly couldn't do tricks like a dog could. Leo couldn't help wishing that things would go back to normal, and everyone would fuss over him instead, but he had a feeling it wasn't going to happen.

But at least Leo had been able to reclaim his place on the sofa, as Mom said she thought it was okay for Leo to sit there when she was feeding Sam, as long as Evie was careful not to let Leo lick him.

"Leo's used to sitting there with you, Evie," she pointed out. "It isn't fair if he's not allowed to anymore. Just keep an eye on him." She sat Sam up to get him to burp, and smiled. "Look, Sam's watching Leo's tail wag. I think he'll love having Leo for company."

Evie scratched Leo behind the ears, and he settled down on her lap, keeping a watchful eye on the baby. He supposed he didn't mind sharing the sofa.

Chapter Four
Tense Times

"Evie! Evie! You're going to be late for school!" Mom was calling up the stairs, sounding angry. She had Sam tucked under one arm, and he was crying. "You won't have time for breakfast!"

Evie stomped down the stairs looking very gloomy. "I don't want any. And I don't want to go to school, either. I don't feel very well. I'm really tired."

Evie's mom took a deep breath and counted to five. "I know. We all are. But it's Friday, and you can sleep in over the weekend."

"If Sam doesn't keep me awake all night, like he did last night," Evie growled.

"It's not his fault, Evie. He doesn't understand the difference between night and day yet." Mom was sounding really exhausted.

"Well, can't you teach him?" Evie looked up at her mom and suddenly grinned. "Oh, all right. I guess not. But I am really, really tired." She sighed and hooked her finger into Sam's tiny hand. "Don't you dare nap all afternoon, Sam. Stay up and then you'll sleep tonight!"

It hadn't been a good week. Evie's dad was back at work now, and it was harder to get everything done without the extra help. Sam was beautiful, but he wasn't sleeping well, and when he was awake he was loud. Everyone's temper was flaring.

Leo was trying his best to keep out of the way, but he never managed to be in the right place. Most days Evie's mom walked into him about three times just doing the laundry. When she got back from taking Evie to school that Friday, she tripped over Leo while she was carrying a basket of laundry, and stepped on his paw, but she didn't seem to be sorry. He held it up and whined, but all she did was snap, "Leo! Not again! Get out of the way, you silly dog!" Leo limped out of the kitchen, feeling very upset.

He sat in the hallway, thoughtfully chewing on a small teddy bear he'd found on the stairs. He just couldn't seem to do anything right anymore. Things had been much nicer before.

At that moment, Sam started crying upstairs and Mom dashed past to go and get him—and saw the small pile of shredded fur that had once been a teddy bear. "Leo!" she wailed, and Leo gazed up at her. He didn't know why she was upset—furry toys were there to be chewed, and he didn't see what the big deal was. But it looked like Mom didn't agree, judging by the way she snatched up what was left of the teddy bear and glared at him.

Leo was still moping when Grandma came by that afternoon, and he was delighted to see her. At last someone who actually had time to sit and scratch him behind the ears properly! He leaned against Grandma's leg affectionately. For a moment he almost wished that she would take him back to her house. Then he shook his head and snorted. No! He was Evie's dog. He was sure that she would get over the baby thing soon, and then maybe they could go back to taking walks and more cuddling.

"You look exhausted!" Grandma was saying to Mom. "Why don't you go upstairs and take a nap? I'll take care of

Sam for you."

Mom sighed. "I'd love to, but he's being so grumpy today. He wouldn't even go to his dad this morning—every time I put him down he howls. I just don't know what's the matter with him. Anyway, I've got to go and get Evie in a minute."

Grandma stood up firmly. "Put him in the stroller and I'll take him with me and get Evie for you. You go and rest. Sam will probably sleep, too."

"If you're sure. . . ." Mom tucked Sam in and set off upstairs, looking grateful.

Me, too! Me, too! Leo whined hopefully, bouncing around Grandma's ankles as she headed for the door. He was still desperate for more walks.

"Sorry, Leo. I'd love to take you,

but I'm not used to this stroller and I can't manage both of you." She looked down at the little dog thoughtfully. "I'd better talk to Evie about you. I don't think she's exercising you enough."

Leo yelped in agreement, and she nodded to herself.

Unfortunately, Grandma's master plan for settling Sam didn't work. At five o'clock, when she had to leave to go home to feed Tigger and Ben, Sam was still wailing. And when Evie's dad walked in at six, he was greeted by a howling baby, a frazzled wife, and an angry daughter.

"Looks like we're in for a fun weekend," he joked, but no one else thought it was funny.

Leo watched Dad hopefully. Mom and Evie had been so stressed by Sam's crying that they had forgotten to feed him. Hc nosed eagerly at his food bowl, and looked up at Dad. He wasn't watching. Leo sighed and trailed back to his basket, where he curled up with his back to thc rest of the family. Maybe he'd better just sleep and try again in a little while.

A couple of hours later, Leo was convinced he was going to starve if he didn't get fed soon. He trotted into the living room, where Mom and Dad were taking turns walking with Sam. Evie was just getting ready to go up to bed. Leo was horrified. If Evie went to bed, they'd never remember to feed him! Desperate measures were needed. He scurried back to the kitchen.

"Oh, thank goodness," Mom whispered, watching as Sam slumped slightly on his dad's shoulder. "He's going to sleep. No, don't stop!"

Dad nodded grimly, and resumed his trek around the room. "I think he's fallen asleep," he sighed, a couple of minutes later. "Can we risk lying him down, do you—"

It was at that moment that Leo trotted back in, carrying his metal food bowl in his teeth. He dropped it hard on the wooden floor and barked.

Sam let out a bloodcurdling wail.

"Leo! You bad dog!" Mom groaned. "That's it. Kitchen! Now! In your basket!" She shooed him out, waving her hands angrily.

Leo was banished. It was the first night he'd ever spent in the kitchen, instead of curled up on the end of Evie's bed. He was so confused. He'd only wanted to eat!

Leo lay in his basket, and stared at the dark kitchen. Why didn't Evie want him upstairs? What had he done?

Didn't she love him anymore?

Chapter Five

Leo in Trouble

The next morning was Saturday, and the family was having breakfast. It was always a really nice time—the beginning of the weekend, when they all had a chance to relax. They usually had something extra-nice for breakfast, too. Today, not even croissants could cheer everyone up.

At least Sam seemed to be in a better

mood. He was lying in his bouncy chair in the living room.

"He's fine," Dad reported back after a quick check. "Seems to be enjoying himself, actually—I think he's learning to bat at that toy you bought him, Evie." He gave a long, slow sigh of relief, and sat down and poured himself a large cup of coffee.

Leo jumped up, his paws on Dad's knee, holding his squeaky bone hopefully in his mouth. Dad was usually good for a game.

"Not now, Leo," Dad muttered, pushing him away gently.

Leo went to paw at Evie's ankles, hoping for a bit of croissant. She dangled a piece by his nose, and he gulped it down gratefully.

"Evie!" Mom said sharply. "Are you giving Leo scraps? How many times have I told you not to feed that dog at the table?" Mom didn't normally mind that much, but today she was tired and cranky.

"Shoo, Leo!" Evie whispered, nudging him out from under the table with her foot.

Leo took one look at Mom's angry face, and trailed sadly into the living room. He sat down next to Sam. The baby was half-smiling at the bouncy animals toy stretched across the front of his chair, and vaguely waving a hand at it every so often. Leo watched. It was fun. He lay down with his nose on his paws and gazed up as the little creatures jumped and danced.

Sam smelled nice—milky—and he was relaxing to be with after the tense, grumpy mood in the kitchen. Sam made little squeaky, grunting noises to himself, and Leo woofed quietly back, his eyes slowly closing as he drifted off for a snooze.

After a few minutes, the jingling of the toy was joined by an irritating buzz. Leo opened one eye. Was it Sam making that noise? Was he supposed to do that? No, Sam was asleep. The buzzing was from a large fly that had landed on the baby's arm. Leo bristled as he watched it crawl over Sam. He hated flies, and he knew Evie's mom did, too; if a fly buzzed nearby, she always shooed it away. That fly should *not* be crawling over Sam.

Leo watched, waiting for his moment to pounce. He was so intent on the fly that he had no idea Evie and her mom had come into the living room to check on Sam. They watched in horror as Leo pounced, his sharp white teeth snapping on the fly—just inches away from Sam's arm.

"Leo, no!" Evie screamed, as her mom threw herself forward to grab Sam away.

Leo had never heard Evie sound like that before—terrified and angry at the same time. He shot under the sofa and lay there, cowering.

Sam hadn't noticed the fly, but he certainly noticed when his mom snatched him out of his sleep. He roared angrily, and waved his arms around.

"Mom, is he okay? I can't believe Leo tried to bite him!" Tears were rolling down Evie's cheeks.

Evie's mom was breathing fast—from where she and Evie had been standing, it really had looked as though Leo had meant to bite Sam's arm, and she'd been terrified. She was pushing up the sleeve of his pajamas, searching for marks, but he seemed fine—just upset at being woken.

"What happened? Are you all right?" Evie's dad rushed into the room, his robe flapping. "Is something wrong with Sam?" he asked, taking in the scene.

"No. No, we're all okay," Evie's mom said slowly.

"Dad, Leo almost bit Sam!" Evie sobbed, throwing her arms around him. She couldn't believe that her sweet puppy would do such an awful thing—but then she'd seen it with her own eyes and watched him jump at her baby brother, teeth bared.

"I don't think he did, Evie." Mom sounded as though she were trying to figure it all out. “Look.”

Lying on the floor next to the bouncy chair was a huge fly, legs in the air, still buzzing faintly.

“You know how Leo hates flies. He’s always snapping at them. I think he just tried to catch a fly that had landed on Sam’s arm.”

Evie lifted her head from where it was buried in her dad’s robe. “Really?”

Evie’s dad was looking serious. “Are you sure?”

“Well, no, I suppose not. But Leo’s never done anything like that before, has he?”

Evie shook her head, smiling in relief. “Never! Oh, Mom, thank goodness you saw that fly—we’d never have known otherwise.”

"Where is Leo?" Dad asked, looking around.

"I shouted at him and he disappeared under the sofa!" Evie went pale. "Oh, he must think we're so angry! Poor Leo." Evie crouched down to look, but Leo flinched away from her, and retreated to the back. Evie sat up, looking hurt. "He won't come," she said miserably.

"You probably need to give him some time." Dad put an arm around her, and the other around Mom and Sam. "Come on into the kitchen."

Leo huddled under the sofa, trembling. No one had ever shouted at him like that before. Evie had behaved as though he'd done something terrible. But he'd been helping Sam! Evie's mom was always saying that flies were horrible, dirty things. She waved them away if they got anywhere near the baby. *Did Evie and Mom think I was trying to bite Sam?* Leo wondered. *I'd never do that! Don't they know I'd never do that?* Leo lay there, feeling confused. No one seemed to understand him very much here anymore. He was always in trouble, and even Evie, who used to love him so much, didn't seem to have any time for him. Maybe they really did think he was the kind of dog who would bite.

"Leo! Lco!" Evie was calling him. She was lying down, peering under the sofa.

"Come out, Leo, please? I didn't mean it. Please come out. I'm so sorry for shouting at you." Her eyes met his hopefully, and Leo couldn't hold back any longer.

He crept forward, tail slowly starting to wag. As he wriggled out from under the sofa, she hugged him tight, burying her face in his thick white fur. “Oh, Leo.” Leo put his paws on her shoulders and licked her face, tasting salt from her tears. Why was she crying? Everything was all right now. He wagged his tail, and licked her again lovingly.

“Ugh, Leo....” Evie giggled and sniffed. “I’m covered in dog drool. Oh, I do love you.” She sighed. “I’m so sorry. I haven’t been showing it much, have I?”

Leo woofed encouragingly. He adored Evie, and he trusted her. Hearing the love in Evie’s voice as he snuggled against her was all he needed to feel better.

Chapter Six

A Difficult Decision

The rest of the day was almost perfect for Leo. Evie seemed to be back to her old self. She cuddled him a lot, and she kept saying she was sorry for thinking he'd hurt Sam, and telling him what a clever dog he was for catching the fly. Just every so often, Leo would remember how upset and angry everyone had been, and shudder, and then Evie would hug him all over again.

Only one thing spoiled it. Leo kept catching worried looks between Evie's mom and dad—worried looks directed at him. Maybe they thought he might still be frightened. He tried to be extra bouncy and friendly, with lots of jumping up to lick them, but it didn't seem to work. If anything, they looked more worried, although they always patted him and smiled.

Evie gave him a huge meal and Leo was so full afterward that he went to sleep on her lap while she was trying to finish her homework at the kitchen table. He didn't notice Evie's parents coming to sit with her, or see the anxious looks on their faces.

"Evie." Mom sounded strangely nervous. "Evie, we have to talk to you, sweetheart."

Evie looked up. "I'm doing it! Look, I'm doing it now. It's only Saturday, Mom. I'll get it done, easily!"

"Not about your homework." Dad's voice was really flat, and Evie looked at him, suddenly scared. This was far more serious than just them complaining that she was rushing through her homework at the last minute.

"It's about Leo," Dad went on.

Her heart suddenly thumping, Evie put her hand down to pet Leo, curled up on her lap. He gave a little whine of pleasure, and stretched out luxuriously in his sleep before curling himself up again even tighter. “What’s the matter?” Evie asked quietly.

Her mom and dad exchanged a look, then her dad sighed. "We're not sure we can keep him, Evie."

Evie gulped, her hand tightening on Leo's neck so that he wriggled uncomfortably. "Why?" she whispered. Then her voice strengthened. "He wasn't biting, Dad, really," she assured him. "He wouldn't do that." She smiled desperately at her dad, knowing she had to convince him.

"Evie, you thought he would," Dad said gently. "And so did your mom. You were so upset this morning."

"But he didn't! It was all a mistake." Evie's eyes were filling with tears. Her dad sounded so set in the decision. She turned to her mom for help, and saw that she was crying, too.

"It's not Leo's fault at all. It's just that we haven't been able to take care of Leo properly, Evie," her mom said shakily. "We all love him, but he needs walks, and lots of attention. He hasn't been getting that. Dogs can get very grumpy if they're cooped up in the house all day."

"I'll walk him more!" Evie cried out. "Every day! Twice a day. I've just been busy with having Sam around, that's all."

"We all have," her dad agreed. "But that's not fair to Leo—he needs a home where he doesn't get forgotten about."

"I didn't mean to!" Evie wailed, so loudly that Leo woke up, his little white head suddenly popping up at the table, making them all giggle hopelessly.

He gave them a happy smile, showing lots of long pink tongue. What was the joke? Then he looked again, turning to sniff at Evie. Maybe there wasn't a joke at all. Something felt wrong. Had he done something bad again? He hunched down onto Evie's lap, looking scared.

"Evie, look at him. He's upset. It's not fair to put him through that," Evie's mom said gently.

Evie sniffed. "If—if we're not going to keep him, what are we going to do? Are you going to give him back to Mrs. Wilson?" She gulped, imagining Leo sitting sadly in the puppy room all on his own, his brother and sisters already gone to new homes.

"No." Dad looked thoughtful. "It would have been the best option, but she's stopped breeding dogs now. She's retired to the seaside, remember?"

"I suppose she might take just Leo back...," Mom said. "Oh, but we don't have her new address."

"I think the sensible thing would be to take him to the animal shelter," Dad said firmly, as though he were trying to convince himself.

"The animal shelter?" Evie's eyes filled with tears again. "Where Grandma got Ben and Tigger? But that's for dogs that people don't want! We *do* want Leo!"

"Dogs that people can't keep, Evie." Mom's voice sounded so sorry that Evie knew there was no point in arguing. Hugging Leo to her, she jumped up and raced up the stairs to her room.

Evie didn't come down for dinner. Leo had already had a huge meal, and he was delighted to stay upstairs with Evie all evening. She was giving him lots of attention, teasing and tickling him, and playing all his favorite games. At bedtime he was allowed to snuggle up on her bed again. Leo heaved a deep, happy sigh. This was where he was meant to be, not down in the kitchen on his own. Everything was the way it should be. He fell asleep at once, worn out from all the playing—so he didn't notice that Evie lay awake half the night, tears rolling silently down her cheeks.

"Evie, you don't have to come."

Leo looked interestedly back and forth between Evie and Dad. They were going somewhere! He padded off to get his leash, and jumped up with his paws on Evie's knees to give it to her.

Evie gulped, and tears started to seep from the corners of her eyes again. He was such a wonderful dog! How could they be doing this? Hurriedly she wiped the tears away—she didn't want Leo to know what was going on. "I'm coming," she said firmly, her voice hardly shaking at all. "I don't want Leo to think I didn't say good-bye."

Dad sighed. "Okay. Hey, Leo, come on, boy. You're going for a car ride," he said, trying to sound cheerful.

But Leo laid his ears back. Something odd was going on. He jumped into the car and saw that Evie's hands were trembling as she fastened his harness. Usually Evie would beg her dad to have the radio on and they'd sing along, but today they hardly spoke at all.

When the car stopped, Leo thought Evie would put his leash on and let him walk, but for some reason she was carrying him up in front of her so she could nuzzle into his fur. Leo licked her face gratefully. He liked being carried, so he could see what was going on. Evie was walking very slowly, though—Dad kept stopping and looking back for her as they headed toward the building. Leo wasn't surprised. It didn't smell good, too clean, a little like the vet's that he'd been taken to a few weeks before.

What was this place?

Evie stood by the reception desk, while Dad explained quietly to a girl in a green uniform. She was nodding sympathetically, and she gave Leo a considering look.

"I'm sure he'll find a new home very quickly. He's a beautiful little dog." She came around the reception desk and held out her arms. "Come on, sweetie," she crooned to Leo.

Leo felt suddenly scared. Who was this girl? Why were they here? All at once he knew that the wonderful, cuddly time he'd been having with Evie over the last day hadn't been real. In fact, nothing had been right since he'd snapped at that fly on Sam's arm. But he still didn't understand! What should he have done? He scrambled helplessly as the girl in green lifted him from Evie's arms. He was squealing with fright, desperately trying to get away.

"Come on, Evie." Her dad quickly marched Evie away, before she grabbed Leo back again. Leo's last sight of Evie was as her dad hustled her out the door, hugging her tightly against him, so that she couldn't turn and see her little dog howling for her to come back.

Chapter Seven
Second Thoughts

As Evie trailed up the front path, she heard someone calling her, and excited woofs. She spun around immediately, thinking that somehow it was Leo.

"Hello, Evie! Ben and Tigger and I are just out for our walk. We thought we'd see if you and Leo wanted to come with us. I know you haven't had a lot of time to walk him lately."

Grandma was beaming at Evie, but then she noticed Evie's dad, who was shaking his head and holding his finger to lips.

"Jack, are you all right?" Grandma asked worriedly, as Tigger and Ben towed her through the gate.

Evie's dad sighed. "Not really."

Evie crouched down to pat Ben and Tigger. "We just took Leo to the animal shelter," she told them quietly. Somehow it was easier to tell the dogs than Grandma. Suddenly she remembered. "You were right, Grandma. You said we wouldn't be able to manage."

"Oh, sweetheart, I'm really sorry." Grandma's face crumpled. "I hadn't realized it was that bad. Why didn't you say something?" she asked Evie's dad.

He shrugged. "It was one of those difficult decisions...," he said sadly. "I'm sure someone really nice will take Leo home. You know that, Evie, don't you?"

Evie was fighting back tears. She didn't want anybody else taking Leo anywhere, even if they fed him out of a solid gold bowl! He was her dog—only he wasn't. Not anymore. In fact, she suddenly realized, she was never going to see him again. She gasped, and then she scrambled up and dashed into the house, tears stinging her eyes.

"That little Westie's still not eating."

"Really? He's only been here three days. He'll change his mind soon."

The two girls in the green uniforms at the animal shelter leaned against the wall, sipping their tea, and staring thoughtfully into Leo's cage. He was curled up at the back, a miserable little ball, not even looking at his overflowing food bowl.

"He's really taking it hard, poor little thing."

"Yeah, I was here when they brought him in—the little girl he belonged to was really upset, too."

Leo snuggled his paws further around his ears to shut out their voices. If he kept his eyes shut tight, he could almost pretend that he was back home.

"Leo! Leo!"

Leo twitched, but it wasn't Evie. It was another of the animal shelter staff, with some people looking for a dog. Quite a few people had been to see Leo already, and everyone said how cute he was. They seemed surprised, as though such a sweet puppy shouldn't really be at a place like this. But when they tried to talk to Leo, and he refused to budge from the back of his cage, they gave up, moving on to friendlier dogs.

"Mom, look at this great dog!" A boy about Evie's age was peering through the cage. "Can we meet him? Please?"

“Sure.” One of the girls who worked at the animal shelter got out her keys. “This is Leo. He’s a beautiful Westie puppy who needs a new home because his owners had a baby and couldn’t keep him. He’s a sweet boy, but he’s not too happy right now. Hey, Leo…,” she cooed gently to him. “Come and meet Ethan. He’s looking for a nice dog just like you.”

Leo hunched himself up tighter. The staff at the shelter were right. He hadn’t accepted what was going on. How could he? He didn’t understand. He couldn’t let anyone take him home, because Evie was coming back for him. He was sure of it. But he was becoming just a little less sure every time he woke up and he was still in a gray concrete cage, waiting for her.

The girl picked him up, and Leo lay limply and sadly in her arms as she carried him out. The little boy petted him gently. "He's great."

Ethan's eyes were shining, just like Evie's used to. Leo let Ethan scratch him behind the ears. That was nice.

"Can we take him home?" Ethan begged.

Home! Leo suddenly twisted in the girl's arms, and growled angrily. What was he thinking? His home was with Evie.

Ethan's parents pulled him away quickly to look at another dog, and the girl with the keys sighed. "Oh, Leo. That would have been a wonderful home. When are you going to let someone else love you?"

Leo slunk back into his cage and curled up facing the wall. He only wanted *Evie* to love him.

Evie thought it was strange that her house could feel so different, just because Leo wasn't there. She didn't have a warm body curled on her toes at night. No cold nose was resting on her knee at mealtimes, hoping for scraps. Only Mom and Sam met her at school, and she and Dad didn't go for walks anymore. Leo's leaving had changed everything.

She tried to explain to Grandma when she went to her house after school on Wednesday.

"I never realized how nice it was having Leo to play with when Mom was busy. She's got so much to do with feeding Sam, and everything. But I had Leo, and it was okay. I really miss him, Grandma." She stared into her juice, and Tigger pushed his head into her lap, sensing that she was unhappy. "Yeah, you miss him, too, don't you, Tigger?"

"I should think your parents miss Leo as well, you know," Grandma said.

Evie nodded miserably. "I think Dad does. I caught him in the hall yesterday with Leo's leash. He looked really confused, and he muttered something about having forgotten. We sometimes used to take Leo for walks after dinner."

"Why don't you talk to them about it? You might have made the wrong decision." Grandma looked thoughtfully at Evie, wondering what she'd say.

Evie petted Tigger. Then she looked up, and her face was so sad that Grandma caught her breath. "I shouldn't ever have let him go, Grandma!" She got up to put on her coat. "I miss Leo so much."

Grandma nodded firmly. "I definitely think you should talk to them." She watched Evie walking slowly down the path, and then looked down at Ben and Tigger. They stared back at her encouragingly. "Mmm. Yes, I think you're right," Grandma muttered to herself.

A couple of times during the week, Evie thought about what Grandma had said, but there didn't seem any point in talking to Mom and Dad about Leo. It would just make everything worse when they said no, and she was sure she wouldn't change their minds. Then on Saturday morning she wandered into the kitchen and found her mom staring at something on the table with a funny look on her face.

"What's the matter?" Evie leaned over to see what she was looking at, and saw that her mom was holding a photo of Leo.

"Oh! Evie, I didn't hear you come in." Mom quickly put the photo back on the windowsill, but Evie was staring at her.

"You miss him, too, don't you?" she asked, her voice suddenly full of hope. "Grandma said you did, but I didn't believe her." Then her shoulders slumped. "But I suppose it doesn't make any difference." She looked over at Sam, who was sitting in his bouncy chair staring in wonder at his toes. She still adored her baby brother, but she couldn't help thinking that it was his fault.

Mom looked, too. "Maybe." Then her voice changed. "Maybe not, Evie. Maybe we were being too hard on him."

"Who?" Dad walked in with the newspaper. "Got you some chocolate, Evie," he added, throwing her a bar.

Evie caught it, but didn't even look to see what kind it was. "Dad, Mom thinks maybe we shouldn't have taken

Leo to the animal shelter!"

Her dad sat down at the table slowly, looking back and forth between them. "Really?" he said thoughtfully.

Mom sat down, too. "Come on. Tell me you haven't missed him."

"But that's not the point! We weren't able to take care of him properly. And what about Sam? Think back to this time last week!"

"I think we overreacted. We panicked—we were all tired, and we made a snap decision. I don't think it was a good one." Mom reached out for his hand. "Leo was such fun to have around. Do you really think he would have hurt Sam?"

Evie watched hopefully, holding her breath as Dad shook his head. "To be honest, I think watching Leo cheered the little guy up sometimes," he said.

They looked over at Sam, who stared back seriously, and said, "Ooooo" in a meaningful way, waving his foot.

"And I really missed taking him to the newsstand this morning," Dad added. "You know, I never came out of the store and found Leo on his own—he was always being petted by someone. Everyone loved him."

Evie took a deep breath. "So can we go and get him back?" she asked, twisting her fingers together anxiously.

Dad looked serious. "It wasn't just about Sam, though, Evie. We'd need to take care of Leo better." He exchanged a glance with Mom. "We need to think this through."

Mom nodded. “Evie, could you do me a big favor and change Sam’s diaper?”

“Now?” Evie asked disbelievingly.

“Yes, now.” Mom smiled at her. “Your dad and I need to talk. And Sam needs a diaper change.”

Evie picked Sam up, making a face, and carried him upstairs.

When Evie got back, Mom and Dad were looking at the photo of Leo again. "Have you decided?" Evie asked hopefully, cuddling Sam close.

"Do you think we can all be better owners for Leo this time around?" Dad asked.

"Yes! And Grandma would help!" Evie reminded him. "She said she would. I could take him out for walks with her and Ben and Tigger."

"No getting grumpy with Leo just because Sam has made us tired."

"No! I promise. Pleeease! Can we have him back?"

Dad grinned at her. "Okay. Let's go and get Leo!"

Evie and her parents were talking excitedly in the car about how great it was going to be to have Leo back, when Dad suddenly stopped in the middle of his favorite story about Leo trying to catch a pigeon.

"I just thought about something," he said quietly. "It's possible someone else has already given Leo a new home. He's been at the shelter a week—and he's such a beautiful dog. Evie, I don't want to upset you, but it's possible Leo's gone."

Evie gulped. "Can you drive faster?"

Evie and her dad jumped out of the car as soon as they got to the animal shelter, while Mom wrestled with Sam and the stroller. "You go!" she said, waving them on.

They dashed into the waiting area, and Dad explained why they had come back, while Evie hopped up and down impatiently. The girl at the desk was taking so long to bring up Leo's file on the computer. At last Evie couldn't stand it. She slipped through the big double door that led to the cages. She had to tell Leo he was coming home!

But Leo wasn't there.

Chapter Eight
Home for Good

"And they wouldn't tell you who'd taken him?" Mom asked indignantly.

"Well, no. I can see why not. We gave Leo up. It wouldn't be fair on his new owners if we could just storm over there and take him back," Dad pointed out.

Mom sighed. "I suppose not. But it seems so unfair."

"Can we not talk about it?" came a small voice from the backseat. Evie was sadly dangling a toy in front of Sam's carseat, and he was giggling, the only member of the family feeling cheerful.

"Sorry, Evie. You're right. It's not going to change anything. At least we're going to Grandma's for lunch—that'll make us feel better. I'll bet she's made a cake."

Evie stared at the car ceiling, concentrating on not snapping at her parents. They were only trying to be nice—but honestly, a cake? That was supposed to make it all right that she'd just lost her beautiful dog forever? Evie sniffed hard. She didn't want to start crying again. She'd finally managed to stop, and her eyes were hurting. She adored Grandma, but she wished they weren't going to her house today. Grandma would never have let anything like this happen to Ben or Tigger, and seeing them was just going to make Evie miss Leo more.

He'll be with a wonderful family, she told herself firmly. He'll be having a great time. The people at the animal shelter wouldn't give him to anyone who wouldn't take care of him well. Someone like us, she couldn't help adding.

Evie had never noticed how many dogs lived in the few streets between her house and Grandma's, but that afternoon they seemed to be everywhere. As they turned the corner onto Grandma's road, she could hear excited yapping, and something tugged in her stomach. It sounded just like Leo. But it was only Ben and Tigger, playing in the front yard. Grandma let them out there somctimes for a change.

Dad put his arm around Evie's shoulders. "You can still come and play with these two, you know," he said sympathetically.

Evie nodded. But it wasn't the same as having her own dog. Although she'd ncver noticed before how much Ben sounded like Leo. It was weird that he had that same squeaky bark. Actually, he probably didn't—she was just going to imagine Leo everywhere for a while. *I wonder how long that will last?* Evie thought to herself miserably. *Forever, I suppose.* She leaned over the gate to undo the latch and the dogs bounded over to say hello.

All three of them.

"Leo!" Evie gasped, finally realizing that the squeaky bark sounded like Leo because it *was* Leo. It was Leo jumping twice his own height to try to get over the gate to greet her. "Leo!" She fought with the latch, but she was crying so much that Dad had to open it for her. Leo shot into her arms and tried to lick her all over, his woofs getting squeakier than ever with excitement.

You came back! You came back! he was saying delightedly, if Evie could have understood him.

"I don't understand," Evie said dazedly, as they sat at the kitchen table. Mom had been right. There was a delicious-looking cake, although at the moment only Leo seemed interested in it. He was perched on Evie's knee, gradually easing himself closer and closer to one of the delicious bits.

Grandma smiled. "Well, after I talked to you, Evie, I changed my mind. I hadn't thought you were ready to have a dog—it's such a huge responsibility. But then with Leo gone, you seemed so sad. And I love Leo, too. I decided that even if you didn't feel you could have him back right now, with Sam so little, then I would keep him myself and you could visit him. Ben and Tigger like having a bouncy young dog to cheer them up." She looked over at her dogs, who were slumped exhaustedly on their cushions, and smiled. Tigger seemed to have his paws over his eyes. "Mmmm. Well, the extra exercise is good for them."

"We can take him home, can't we? He can live with us, like Grandma said. And Grandma can help us out if we're having a problem?" Evie asked her parents anxiously.

"Definitely!" said her dad. "Leo's part of the family. Aren't you, boy?" Then he laughed. "And Sam thinks so, too."

Sam was sitting on Mom's lap, next to Evie and Leo. He was leaning over toward Leo, his fingers clumsily batting at Leo's shiny collar tag, so that it jingled and flashed in the sun. Sam gurgled happily, enjoying his game. Leo shook his ears and snorted gently, edging slightly closer on Evie's knee so Sam could reach.

Evie smiled down at him, hugging him tightly. Leo knew that he was home for good.

Holly Webb started out as a children's book editor, and wrote her first series for the publisher she worked for. She has been writing ever since, with more than 100 books to her name. Holly lives in England with her husband, three young sons, and several cats who are always nosing around when she is trying to type on her laptop.

For more information
about Holly Webb visit:

www.holly-webb.com

www.tigertalesbooks.com